MOSAIC

A TOMMY SHORE MYSTERY

LAWRENCE DORFMAN

ROUGH
EDGES
PRESS

Mosaic
Paperback Edition
Copyright © 2022 Lawrence Dorfman

Rough Edges Press
An Imprint of Wolfpack Publishing
5130 S. Fort Apache Rd. 215-380
Las Vegas, NV 89148

roughedgespress.com

Paperback ISBN 978-1-68549-134-5
eBook ISBN 978-1-68549-133-8
LCCN 2022942376

MOSAIC

"Don't make a career out of underestimating me."
—James Ellroy, *The Big Nowhere*

PROLOGUE

I stayed alone in my apartment for almost the entire isolation as the pandemic picked up, venturing out to walk the streets only once or twice a week. The destinations varied between The Wine Thief liquor store on Crown Street, the organic market on State Street, and when I got annoyed at the prices at the market, the bodega across the street from the apartment.

I could get basic stuff from the bodega. Their prices were also high but it felt more like I was contributing to the well-being of a family rather than to a conglomerate. The bodega owner had done his best to comply with the state's edicts, including putting up a plastic partition between the clerk and the customers, but it still felt vaguely dangerous buying there. The street people used the place pretty regularly, and I found myself wondering if they had access to the facilities needed to be safe--wash basins and paper towels, and the like. I refused to carry a bottle of Purell around with me, mostly because I couldn't find any, and the one they supplied at the counter never had much left in it.

It had been six months since the virus changed the world and over 10 months since my last case. That one rocked me pretty good.

I had been hired by an exotic dancer to find and stop a stalker who'd gotten backstage at the club where she worked and was making her life miserable.

By the end, she and her boyfriend both suffered horrible, violent deaths that sent me into a deep tailspin for weeks after. I spent a lot of time drinking alone, and it still haunted me. That case had spun out of control very quickly and involved blackmail and the underworld of New Haven. I tried to protect her and do the job she hired me for, but deceit and lies and double crosses on all sides cropped up each way I turned and made it impossible.

I hadn't seen very much of my drinking buddy, Reilly, during the "before" period and, of course, nothing at all after. He seemed to have gone underground. I knew his involvement in that case took a toll on him as well. I called him a number of times to go out, but each time he was either busy or "under the weather." I knew from his sister that the doctors still hadn't found out what was actually wrong with him and that they had been putting him through a series of painful and costly tests. Whatever he had left him listless and tired and a prime candidate to pick up whatever this "plague" was. When it started, he holed up in his apartment and never left, ordering food and booze deliveries almost daily.

I had my own way of dealing with it. Hunkered down, I caught up on a ton of reading, even re-reading books that I loved from my previous life in the book business. The pile by the bed had gotten completely unwieldy so it was a welcome distraction to finish one and actually shelve it. I drew the line at alphabetizing.

Otherwise, I spent the rest of the days staring at my phone or looking stuff up on my ancient laptop, where I read stats about the progression of the disease and the effects it was having on New Haven, on Connecticut, on the country, and on the world. It got to be an obsession.

Recovery was a slow-go in Connecticut, with only a handful of bars and restaurants willing to go back to what they had been before. People were still wary being around large groups, and many still wore masks when they ventured outside.

That morning, I was sitting in my leather easy chair reading the *New Haven Register* and eating a bacon, egg, and cheese sandwich that I'd picked up from the takeout window of Meat & Co. on a morning walk around the block. I had re-upped the advertisement for my services just two days prior and was looking for my ad in the paper. The lead story was about a group of people in Wallingford who called themselves the Knights of The Message. They were protesting outside the giant Walmart there, unhappy that the rehiring there had been given to minority workers. It didn't matter that the store brought people back by seniority. According to the signs the protestors carried, it was a travesty of epic proportions, and they weren't, by God, going to stand for it.

I shook my head and laughed. I had been aware of the fringe groups that made up some of the more rural areas of the state but always considered Wallingford to be a fairly level-headed town. It was mostly blue collar but certainly a lot more liberal than some of the border towns in the northern part of the state. Looking at the Confederate flags the people were carrying in the newspaper picture, it occurred to me there must also be a large number of transplanted folks who moved up to Connecticut from below the Mason/Dixon line. Either that or they were really bad at following directions.

I stopped reading when the landline rang, the number I had advertised. I picked up immediately.

"Tommy Shore. World-Class Sleuth. How can I help you?"

There was hesitation on the other end. Perhaps my greeting was overly optimistic. I tried again.

"Hello? This is Tommy."

I heard a sigh and then a woman's voice. "Mr. Shore, my name is Carla Vitter. I need to hire you to find my brother-in-law. He's been missing for over a week. Is this a good time?"

I looked towards the heavens, sending up a silent "Thank you." I'd eventually end up thinking "Be careful what you ask for."

PART 1

ONE

There was no easy way to get to Wallingford from downtown New Haven. You could take I-91 to exit 15, but then you still have to follow the side roads all the way back to the one main road, Route 5. Or you could go north from downtown and follow Whalley Avenue all the way out, pick up the Merritt Parkway in Amity, and deal with a hundred lights. I opted for the latter. It would give me an opportunity to survey the landscape. Besides, there was a decent Jewish deli that made passable corned beef sandwiches if I went that way. Hopefully, they re-opened or would at the very least be doing takeout.

When Carla Vitter called me, I was doing what most of the world was doing: trying to decide how involved I could safely be out in society. Social butterfly had never been my forte even before then. I was fairly certain that it wasn't going to change all that much as things opened up a bit. I needed to work. It had been nearly a year. I lived off the money I had made from that case and then from savings, but I was now down to the remnants of my relief check.

It still amused me about the coincidence of it all. I had been reading about Wallingford in the paper when my client called and asked to hire me. It was not typical for me to go out to a client's home before I was officially hired. I was used to getting some advance money, but these were unusual circumstances. Carla had laid out the basics of her situation and I was intrigued. Being broke opens doors to all sorts of possibilities.

Carla had been babysitting her sister's daughter. The sister was killed in a car accident a few years earlier, and the little girl was being raised by her father, Earl Scosa, a single dad who lived near Carla and her husband in Wallingford. Earl hadn't been seen in more than a week, and according to Carla, the local police weren't being cooperative. She was at her wit's end and didn't know where else to turn.

Wallingford was like many of the small industrial towns that made up much of Connecticut. There was the predictable town green in the area known as downtown, but most of the businesses were on the main drag, Route 5, in a series of strip malls that eventually melted into the larger town of Meriden to the north.

Like many towns of its ilk, Wallingford was once a thriving community, known for producing silver products. When silver became a valuable commodity, priced far beyond the reach of most consumers, many of the businesses started to leave. The powers-that-were at the time tried to attract business from the high-tech sector and were moderately successful until, once again, those businesses left for greener pastures. Now Wallingford was a blue-collar town with a large number of car dealerships, a Super Walmart, and very little else.

I programmed Carla's address into the GPS on my phone.

It was a beautiful Wednesday in early July. The weather had finally decided to cooperate after being difficult in April and May and spotty in June. The sky was clear, a brilliant blue, and the heat that typically overwhelmed New England in the summer was staying reasonable.

I rented a car from the Hertz place on State Street and took my time driving through New Haven, trying to get a sense of which places had reopened and which were still closed or gone altogether. There were a number of Op-Ed columns recently about the devastation that the virus was wreaking on retail, but it looked at first glance that many of the stores had opened again, at least partially. I went up Chapel Street and then over to Whalley Avenue. I planned to get my breakfast sandwich at the deli before I headed north on the Merritt.

It felt good to see people out again, and there were definitely more cars on the road. Many of the folks I saw walking the streets were still wearing face masks, the "new normal." I hated that phrase when every newspaper reporter or television broadcaster used it during the isolation period, but it was starting to make more sense now.

When I got to the deli, it was open, but they were limiting the number of people who could enter the store at one time. I waited outside for a few minutes until the young girl who was working the door waved me in. I looked around and saw people sitting at a few of the tables on the left side of the restaurant and one older couple sitting on the right. There was no one at the counters. I'd read that restaurants could make their own choices on how to operate but that most were only allowed to bring in half of their capacity, unless they had outdoor seating. I thought about my friends in the business who were still struggling.

A scruffy looking guy behind the counter, maybe 25 years old, barked, "Next!" at me loudly. It took me out of my daydream. I could see he was impatiently waiting for me to order.

"Do you know what you want or do you need to see a menu? Got other customers waiting."

I looked back outside and chuckled. There was one guy standing outside, and he was on his phone. The guy at the counter was losing the whole kumbaya-ness of it all and had gotten back in touch with his inner rude boy. I decided to be difficult.

"Hmm...not really sure if I want corned beef or pastrami...it's been so long, and it's just so hard to choose. I mean, I really like them both. What do you think? Does one look better than the other or are they both the same? Hard to tell, right? So tough to make up my mind..."

I stopped short of drawling out my questions to purposely take my time, and kept looking straight at him until he finally averted his eyes. He got the point and asked again, this time without the tone.

"I think they're both really good. Do you have a preference?"

I ordered the corned beef and asked for an extra pickle and a Dr. Brown's cream soda. He put the order in, and I paid then moved to the side to wait. The order came out quickly, and the kid handed me the bag, saying that he threw in a few extra pickles. I nodded, gave him a big smile, and left.

I had planned to eat half of it on the drive up and the other half on the way back, but it was so delicious that I ended up devouring it before I got off the highway. The GPS directed me to exit 65, and I exited to a stop sign, then turned right toward the center of town.

Things changed immediately the farther I got from the parkway. Beat-up old colonials and two-family houses in dire need of repairs seemed to make up many of the neighborhoods I passed through. There were people out in front of many of them, working on cars and pick-up trucks or just sitting on beach chairs and watching as cars passed by. I assumed that they were also waiting for local businesses to reopen. Connecticut was one of the last to lift the quarantine ban, and many people had yet to go back to work

After a series of left and right turns, I pulled up in front of Carla's house. It was a beige two-family deal badly in need of painting. A small Kia was parked on the unpaved driveway. There was a Big Wheels trike in front and various toys scattered around the small piece of ground that was probably called the front yard by the occupants. I got out and started up the sidewalk.

"Are you the police?"

The small voice seemed to come from nowhere but as I looked around, I could see the face of a child peeking around the corner of the porch. I stopped walking towards the steps.

"I'm not. Are you?"

I could hear a laugh.

"No, silly, I'm just little."

I laughed back, feigned looking around, and responded, loudly, "Who said that?"

A very young girl came from around the corner of the porch and stopped about six feet away from me. She was adorable, maybe six or seven years old, with an angelic face, a big smile, and a cascade of blonde ringlets that fell past her shoulders. Under her right arm was a floppy doll, a Raggedy Ann or whatever today's equivalent might be. The little girl's left hand was flat against her face, as if to say she wasn't sure whether she should talk to the stranger in the yard or run away. Her curiosity got the best of her. The questions came quickly.

"Me. I said it. Shana. Who are you? Are you here to see my Aunt Carla? Do you know where my daddy is? Do you work with him?"

I smiled, staying where I was and keeping both hands down at my sides. I wanted her to see that I was not a threat.

"Hi there. My name is Tommy. Your Aunt Carla called me on the phone and asked me to come see her. I don't know where your daddy is but I'm going to try and find him so I can talk to him. Is that okay?"

I could see her trying to grasp my answers when the front screen door opened and a woman's voice called her by name.

Shana scurried in front of me and ran up the rickety stairs, then grabbed onto the legs of the woman in the doorway. I assumed this was Carla. She frowned and asked, "Mr. Shore?"

She stood there and watched me. I nodded and moved toward the stairs but she put her hand up to stop me.

"Do you have an ID?"

I considered how to answer the question. I had never gotten an official license, mostly because the state's fees were high and because I wanted to keep my prices affordable for folks who couldn't afford a real investigator but still needed help. I considered getting a fake badge to flash. Most people don't look that close, and it would give some peace of mind, fake or not. I took out my AAA card with my name on it from my wallet and showed it to her.

"Hi Carla, Tommy Shore. I actually don't have my PI license with me but I do have this, so you can see that I'm who I say I am. Either that or I have Tommy's wallet."

She didn't laugh at the lame joke, but I saw her considering it. The fact that I'd used her name seemed to put her at ease slightly. She decided to take the chance that I was who I said I was.

"Okay, come inside."

I went up the stairs to the porch and followed her in. She occupied the first-floor apartment, and the front door to the right of the porch opened directly into the living room. There was an old wooden coffee table in front of an old couch that had a simple jigsaw puzzle under construction on it. The puzzle's frame was complete, and the pieces were in a pile in the top lid of the box the puzzle came in. Carla gently sat the little girl down on the couch and told her to keep working on it. I followed Carla through the small room and through a connecting door, partially blocked by the television set, into a tiny kitchen. There was a small Formica table with three chairs around it, the fourth side of the table butting up against a side window. The only things on the table were a set of Elvis salt and pepper shakers and a stack of paperwork. A quick glance told me the papers were mostly bills and dunning letters.

I took the chair to the right, jockeying sideways to fit myself between the table and the narrow counter behind it, where a microwave and toaster sat next to a loaf of Wonder Bread and a package of off-brand English muffins.

"Can I offer you some coffee, Mr. Shore?"

I glanced quickly at the counter by the sink where a small Mr. Coffee machine and a can of Folgers sat. My inner coffee snob got the best of me and I declined.

"Tommy. Call me Tommy. No, I'm fine. Maybe a glass of water?"

People like to think they're being a good host, and I wanted her to be relaxed and comfortable with me.

She turned to the cupboard above the sink and reached in for a glass, turning on the tap at the same time. She took down a jelly glass with flowers on it from a shelf, then waited a few seconds until she filled it from the tap. When she turned to hand it to me, I could see she was trying hard to hold back tears.

I took the glass, thanked her, asked her to sit down, and took out my pad and pen.

Carla appeared to be in her early 40s, but her face didn't hide the fact that many of those years must have been tough ones. She was wearing a plain blue dress that had clearly seen better days and kept it buttoned up in the front almost to the top, with a little bit of open neck exposed. I could see a largish cross alongside a small locket, the kind that usually held a picture inside. She seemed to be carrying the weight of the world on her shoulders.

"Carla, how about you tell me everything that's been going on and what you need and then we can try to figure out what we might be able to do?"

She looked at me for a few seconds, looked at the pad, then nodded and sat down in the chair opposite me. I sipped the tepid water and waited as she stared out the window for a minute or so. When she looked at back at me, she inhaled deeply and began telling me the story.

TWO

"Mr. Shore, I called you because I don't know what else to do. Like I mentioned on the phone, we haven't seen my brother-in-law, Earl Scosa, in over a week. He left my niece Shana with us last Tuesday, saying he had some business he needed to attend to. He told me he'd only be gone a few days but that he would call me regularly to check in on her. Well, he called me once the day after he left and there's been nothing since. It's unusual. He's not the type to run off. He's completely devoted to his daughter. I got worried and called the police last Friday, but they said it's a low priority for them, given what's been going on with the Coronavirus. They said they were short-staffed and that I should give it a few more days, so I waited until Monday and called again. At that point, they basically said they would try but only get back to me if they had something. I just didn't want to wait any longer, so I called you when I saw your ad."

She paused to catch her breath. She seemed distracted and kept looking out the window at the street, like she was watching for something. I could hear Shana singing to herself in the living room. I tried to gently prod Carla to finish telling me the story but got the sense that she was going to take her time. I figured that she probably hadn't had much company in a while and would take advantage of having someone here now, listening to the whole story.

"Go on."

She looked at me and her eyes were moist.

"I'm sorry, Mr. Shore. It's really been a trying few months. My husband Paul and I were struggling before, but when this virus thing happened, it really set us back. We were barely getting by on what he made at his job, and then he lost it back in February at the start of the pandemic. He's only now getting unemployment, but it's barely enough to pay the bills, let alone have anything left over for extras. To add insult to injury, our tenants upstairs left unexpectedly, owing us three month's rent. We're waiting for a second stimulus check. I intend to pay you out of that."

I tried to keep any kind of emotion off my face. I definitely needed the cash but knew I would have a hard time convincing myself that to take much money from these folks. Even if I pro-rated my fee and got them some kind of an answer in a week, it would run at least a thousand dollars. I pushed those thoughts to the side and prompted her to continue.

"Tommy, Carla. Please call me Tommy. My dad was Mr. Shore. I completely understand what you're going through. Just finish telling me everything you know."

She took another deep breath and went on.

"I think I told you that my sister Janet, Shana's

mom, died a few years back. She was killed in a horrible car accident while coming home from work late one night. It was a hit and run. From what the police could find out, her car had been forced off the Merritt, hit from behind, and she lost control. Her car went down an embankment and hit some trees. They said she died instantly, but the fact that she didn't suffer brought me very little comfort, and they never found out who was in the other car. A different car stopped to help, and that driver said he seemed to remember the make of the hit-and-run car, but no one was ever found or charged. We asked the insurance company for money to bury her, but they kept stalling us, and after a few months, told us they wouldn't pay a dime. Said this was a no-fault state and claimed that she had been drinking. My sister was a virtual teetotaler, Mr. Shore. She never drank to excess. She couldn't afford to. In the end, we didn't have the money to get a lawyer and sue, so we ended up letting it go. We had to borrow money from my other sister for the funeral."

It didn't make sense to me, but I wrote it all down. I interrupted her to ask a question.

"Can I ask, what does your husband do?"

The question seemed to surprise her.

"He's a locksmith. He had his own company here in Wallingford for years, but there were some personal issues, and he ended up having to close it. He went to work for a bigger company out of West Hartford until, like I said, he got furloughed in February. Why do you ask?"

"Just trying to get as much information as possible. In this line of work, you never know what might help towards figuring out what's going on. Please continue?"

She held up a finger and got up, going to the kitchen door to look in on Shana. "You okay, baby? Why don't you turn the TV on and watch 'pa Pig'?"

I heard a muted response and some movement, then cartoon voices. Carla clearly wanted to keep Shana from hearing our conversation. When she came back to the table and sat down, she spoke to me in hushed tones.

"The thing is, both Paul and I believe Earl was into something. We have no idea what it was, but we know it wasn't anything good. He had gotten secretive lately and was keeping a very low profile around here. Sometimes he would leave Shana here all day, then call me up and plead for her to sleep over here. That happened at least once or twice a week. Now, don't get me wrong, I love that child as if she was my own, but it was clear as a bell that something wasn't right."

I looked at her and could see she was still quite angry about it. I changed my tack.

"What does Earl do for a living?"

She sat back and folded her arms.

"That's the thing...he really didn't have a job where he would have been working all those late hours. Years ago, just after he and my sister got married, he tried getting in to the state police but flunked out of the academy. Since then, I know he's done a number of different jobs. Salesman, landscaping...he was painting houses for a while...but the last job I know of was working as a driver for one of those companies that pick up the older people who are on state care and taking them to their doctor's appointments. It was a company that was like Uber, where you work for yourself? They gave him magnetic stickers that went on the sides of the car...what was the name? Veyo, I think it was. He would start out at five o'clock in the morning and go until six at night. I didn't think he was happy doing that. He had to use his own car and pay for his own gas. Plus, a lot of the people that he had to pick up were drug users who needed rides to the methadone clinics. Not the most reliable kind of people."

I nodded. "Do you happen to know the kind of car he drove? Maybe the make or the model?"

She grimaced. "Well, Janet's car had been totaled and I know he was using the Malibu. A Chevy Malibu. It was older...I think they bought it new in 2013, maybe? I really don't know a lot about cars, Mr. Shore."

I could see she was getting anxious. I wondered if her husband knew that she had contacted me.

"That's fine. I can find out. Just a few more questions, Carla, and that'll be it. Do you know if Earl had any other vices, like gambling or drugs or drinking? Do you know of any places where he might have hung out, a bar or a club or the casinos maybe?"

She shook her head.

"No, Earl didn't do any of that stuff. He was like a boy scout. My sister was the same way. Neither of them had any kind of vices like that. They went to church every Sunday, First Congregational on Main Street. She worked for the elementary school part-time and had a second job at Foucault Appliances. There wasn't any money for extras. They saved up and went to Disney World once when Shana was three. Drove the car all the way down to Florida, for God's sake. I wasn't sure the car would make it."

She paused as if a thought had occurred to her.

"I will say this. He changed after Janet got killed.

He became so angry that you couldn't have a conversation with him. He'd start screaming about this group or that group. Didn't care who knew it. He was mad at the world for what happened to my sister. I can't say that I blame him...losing your wife like that. Before that, he lived for Janet and Shana, but afterwards he was a completely different person."

She leaned in to whisper, conspiratorially.

"I've half a mind to tell you that I think he got involved with one of those hate groups here, you know, those white power people. When he would come by to pick Shana up and I would bring her out to the car, I could see signs and materials in the back. He would never let me strap her in to her car seat, always had to do it himself. The signs were usually covered up, but I could see a little bit poking through sometimes and that's when I realized what they were. Words like PURITY and the like written on them."

She looked outside again and was twisting a small piece of cloth she picked up off the counter.

"Mr. Shore, I don't know who killed my sister, but I know Earl was always looking for someone to blame. Wallingford has certainly changed over the last few years, and there's a larger population of minority folks living here now. It's stirred up some folks who have lived here a long time and don't like the change."

I nodded, said I understood, then stood up.

"Carla, what I'm going to do is ask around about Earl and see if I can't get some idea about where to start looking. There's not really a whole lot here to go on, but it's a place to start. I'll see what I can dig up and look into that other stuff as well, see if he joined any special interest groups. If I think there's a case I can help with,

I'll call you and we can figure it out things from there. Sound okay?"

She was looking out the window again but then turned toward me and I could see the toll that the sadness of her life was taking on her.

"I'm really at wit's end, Tommy. I really don't know what to do. When I saw your ad, I thought you might be someone who could help me get some answers. Will you help? I promise that I'll find a way to pay you. Like I mentioned, we have a check from the government coming any day now, but if push comes to shove, I can maybe sell some of my mother's jewelry if I have to. There's not much there, but it could be enough."

I moved closer to her and put my hand on her shoulder. I felt her tense a little, so I removed it and took a step back.

"Let's not worry about that now. I'll see what I can find out and call you when I get something. The money can wait. Besides, I know where you live."

I regretted the lame joke as soon as I said it. I kept smiling, hoping she would see that I was teasing. I moved toward the living room, and Carla got up and followed. Shana was still working on the puzzle during the commercials.

"Bye, Shana." I waved at her, she smiled back at me, and waved.

I walked out of the house, got in my car, and headed back toward the Merritt. I didn't like the feeling in my gut and was hoping that at least one of the bars in New Haven was open for business.

THREE

The drive back to New Haven was uneventful. I got off the parkway in North Haven and found my way over the back streets so I could pick up I-95, then took the downtown exit once I got into New Haven. After turning in the rental, I started walking toward the Trinity Bar.

I was worried that Trinity wouldn't survive the pandemic. There had been a huge fire in the apartment above the bar three years before, and the owners were forced to shut it down completely until the building was brought back up to code. Once that was done, the state then made them jump through all kinds of ridiculous bureaucratic hoops to get their licenses back. Still, they persevered and reopened about a year ago, doing a solid business ever since. When the virus hit and the owners decided not to try and do curbside takeout with their food business, they were forced to furlough most of the staff. The bar had recently re-opened, and hopefully the folks that worked there were able to come back to their jobs. I had grown quite fond of many of them.

It was a nice three block walk. Many of the stores were still closed down in this part of town, but the Dunkin' Donuts was open, as was Evolution Tattoos. I glanced inside as I passed and could see the artist sitting in the chair, smoking a cigarette and looking at a magazine. Guess people were still a little wary about doing anything where close contact and blood were involved.

I crossed over in the middle of the block and went down a back alley behind the Elm City Market, jockeying around the bike racks and the courtyard tables to go in by the side door.

Once inside, I waited a few seconds for my eyes to adjust to the darkness. Looking toward the full bar on the left, I could see Lindsay wiping down glasses. I ambled over and sat down at the end of the bar. She saw me and her face lit up.

"Tommy! Finally! I thought I'd never see you again. How the hell are you? What'll you have, the usual?"

Lindsay was what used to be known as a great broad. She was a terrific bartender, but she didn't suffer fools easily and could give as good as she got. It was great to see her.

"Lindz! You are definitely a sight for sore eyes. Been far too long and yes, I thought it would never end. I would definitely love a double Jameson."

She put a short glass down in front of me and grabbed a half-full bottle of Jameson from the shelf behind her, pouring the liquid gold in one fluid move into the glass and putting it down in front of me. I watched as she backed up a few feet. Not quite the socially distant six, but I was okay with it. Just glad I didn't have to try and drink through a mask. I took a sip, closed my eyes, and sighed.

"Ah, finally home."

She laughed, and we caught each other up on what went on since the last time we were together. Her story was similar to the one I would eventually hear from almost everyone – grocery shopping, Netflix, catching up on reading, and boredom. With the occasional walk around the block thrown in for good measure.

Another customer came in and sat at the other end of the bar. She left to take care of him, so I pulled out my phone, opened up Google, and brought out my pad to go over my notes.

I'd written down that Veyo was the last place Earl had worked, so I typed it into the phone. A ton of information came up immediately.

Veyo was a medical transportation company tied into Medicaid. They used an app that their drivers downloaded to signal when a client needed a ride. A driver would accept the job and get paid a stipend for every trip they made. Basically, Uber with a steadier customer base. The company started in Arizona a few years back and was now located in four states. Connecticut was one of the more recent states to offer it. There was a link on the site to fill out the forms to apply to become a driver. I clicked on it, and it took me to a series of questions. I filled them out, deciding that I would go see what the whole thing was about, in hopes that one of the drivers or the facilitator might know or remember something about Scosa. It was a long shot but there wasn't much else to go on. When I was done, I received an immediate notification that the next meeting was that night at 5:00 in the basement of an office building in North Haven. I checked the box confirming that I would attend.

Lindsay came back down to my side of the bar. I could see through the window openings behind the bar that more people had come in and were sitting in the booths, holding lunch menus. It reminded me that I was hungry. It had been hours since my corned beef sandwich.

They made a terrific burger here, so I ordered one from Lindsay. She topped off my drink and left to put in my food order.

I googled the town of Wallingford's police department public relations phone number and called it. I got a recording:

"Due to the recent Covid-19 limitations, appointments with this department must be made in writing via email. Once received, we will get back to you as quickly as possible." An email address followed.

I laughed as I listened. Every town, no matter the size, was now bogged down in even more bureaucratic red tape than ever. I would have to go there in person.

I couldn't afford to keep renting a car, so I scrolled through my contact list, looking for friends that I could borrow one from. I ended up calling Mark, an old friend I'd known for 35 years. We'd met during my short stint in the music business and had stayed close, going to concerts or meeting for breakfast as regularly as possible. He was a musician who traveled a lot, playing venues in places as far away as Nashville and Cleveland, and his car often sat in his driveway when he was away. I took a shot that he had started working again. I knew that many of his gigs had been cancelled during the pandemic but that others had only been postponed. If that was the case and he was going to be out of town, I could use his car. He picked on the first ring.

"Yo, Tomás. Just thinking about you this morning. We're overdue for breakfast. What's shakin'?"

We had developed a shorthand speak over the many years of our friendship.

"All good. Might have a case. You workin'? Need a car for a week or so."

There was slight hesitation, and I could hear pages being turned.

"Your lucky day, got a gig Friday in Jersey. Taking the train to NYC and gonna Uber out from there. So, good to go. Come by and get it. Whenever. I'll leave keys inside, under the seat."

He lived a few miles away, out in Hamden.

"Muchas. Be out later today. Full tank of gas and breakfast on me next time."

I hung up just as Lindsay brought out the food and placed it in front of me. The burger was perfectly cooked, pink inside, with burnt grilled onions, just how I like it. On occasion, the onions would give me agita, but it was worth it.

Lindsay stayed down at my end of the bar. I could tell there was something bothering her that she wanted to talk about. Best to get it out of the way so I could eat in peace.

"What's up?"

She furrowed her brow. "Have you seen Reilly recently? He hasn't come in here yet. Staying away this long has to be hard, so I was betting he'd be here as soon as we re-opened but nothing. You two have a falling out?"

I shook my head. I didn't want to engage in this conversation with her but knew she wouldn't just let it go. I put down the burger and looked at her.

"Nope, not at all. Just haven't seen much of him. He went underground when the Covid thing started, and I'm not sure he's come out yet. I called him a couple of times, but it always goes to voicemail and he hasn't called me back yet. I'm pretty sure he has caller ID so he knows it's me. I considered going over there to see what's up but then thought screw it, he knows where to find me."

I was vaguely aware the last bit sounded like a snubbed girlfriend, but I didn't really care much anymore. Must be the "new normal." Lindsay read the signs, shrugged, and moved down to the other end of the bar to see if her other customers needed anything. I finished eating, tossed a twenty on the bar, and walked out, heading back to my apartment.

Taking my time on the walk uptown, I peered into almost every shop I passed to see what their stories might be. Most of the people working in the stores were wearing protective masks, and almost every checkout counter held multiple bottles of hand sanitizer. No store had many customers in it.

There were still only a few restaurants that would let many people dine inside. The state dictated 50 percent capacity, and some places had created outdoor dining spaces on the sidewalks. There was a smattering of folks eating at those tables. I looked at people as I passed and could see many of them furtively glancing back my way, trying to make sure I kept the proper distance. I sighed and wondered how long it would be before that particular interaction ceased. Probably never.

Coming around the corner to my apartment, I looked over to see if the Owl Bar had re-opened fully. I crossed the street to look inside and could see that the lights were on, but they were still only selling cigars and coffee upfront, using a skeleton staff. During the quarantine, they experimented with "mixed drink kits" that could be used to make cocktails, replete with the kind of miniature bottles that you got on airlines. Nips. I questioned how successful it would be when I heard about it, but they stopped doing it shortly after they started. The liquor stores had been deemed "essential" during the crisis, so you could get full bottles of anything you needed for a lot cheaper. Guess the owner overestimated his customer's buying into the convenience of not having to walk around the block.

I crossed back over and went into my building. The inside security door was being held open by a metal stopper on the floor. I stopped short but then realized that the threat of touching the security keypad must now be considered worse than the threat of anyone breaking and entering. I shook my head and went to my apartment.

Once inside, I looked around the place. I'd spent weeks staring at the walls and was excited at the possibility of a new case. But today's meeting with Carla took some of the wind out of my sails, and I knew I could easily let myself slide into a funk. I tried to shake it off but kept seeing Shana's face in my head. I knew I would take the case, money or not. The white knight had returned to haunt me.

FOUR

I changed my clothes, putting on a slightly dressier shirt and some dark dress pants, then called for an Uber on the app. It told me I had seven minutes until it arrived, so I downed a glass of orange juice, ice cold from the fridge. I wanted the sugar rush for what I knew would be a long and tedious endeavor, sitting through an hour or more of instructions on becoming a Veyo driver. I rinsed the glass, locked up, and went out front to wait.

The Uber was on time but upon getting in, I was immediately confronted with the overwhelming aroma of very powerful cologne. The cheap kind. I had my virus mask around my neck, so I pulled it up over my mouth and nose. The driver, a white kid who looked to be around twenty and wore his hair up in gnarled Rasta braids, watched me get in and pull the mask up. He turned down the reggae that was playing and spoke to me through his rearview mirror.

"Hey, bud, you don't really need that anymore. I wipe the car down after every passenger. No Corona here."

I looked back at him in the mirror and shook my head. There was a time I would have made a comment but I didn't have the will to engage anymore. I fell into virus-speak.

"No worries. As much for you as it is for me. All good."

He shrugged and headed down College Street to take the highway into Hamden. I was happy he chose the faster route. There would be fewer lights he might have to stop at. I was also pleased that he had a heavy foot. We got to Mark's house quickly. Small blessings. I got out and he sped off.

The car I was borrowing was parked in front of the small cape where Mark lived with his girlfriend. She was a nurse at Yale-New Haven hospital and worked shifts that changed constantly. She had been on the front lines through much of the crisis, one of the unsung heroes. There was no one home now, but as he'd told me, the keys were in the car under the driver's seat. It was a small Chevy Cruze, and I had to adjust the seat back to get in easily. Once in, it started right up, and I drove back down to the main road and headed toward North Haven.

The building where the sign-up meeting would be was one of those nondescript white offices. These types of structures went up quickly in the 1980s, and each one looked the same. Stuck in the ground just in front of the building was a small hand-made sign that someone had hand-printed "Veyo" on, with a red arrow pointing toward the rear parking lot. I turned into the entrance and followed the driveway along the building until I saw other cars, finding the last open space in front of a decrepit fence. I backed in, got out, and used the fob to lock the car door.

There were two back entrances, one that went into the ground floor offices and one that led to a staircase down to the basement offices. I followed the sign pointing down. At the bottom of the staircase were two bathrooms, one for each gender, so I went into the men's room to check how I looked and to wash my hands. It hadn't quite become an obsession yet, but I found myself taking advantage of any opportunity that presented itself. When I was finished, I left and followed a series of hallways toward the back offices, where I could hear the low murmur of a small crowd.

I saw immediately that I didn't have to worry about my attire. A quick look around the room at the people waiting for the seminar showed me that most of these folks weren't all that concerned about dressing for success. Most were sitting on folding chairs, but a few stood against a back wall. All eyes turned to look at the newcomer.

No one seemed to be talking to anyone else, and most were busying themselves with filling out the application. The ages ran the gambit from a kid who looked to be in his late teens wearing an "Ozzy" t-shirt to an elderly man with a cane on which he balanced an old-fashioned newsboy cap. No one wore a mask.

At the front of the room was a man in his late 40s, holding a clipboard and handing out magnetic signs that drivers would stick on both sides of their cars. There were two people in line ahead of me, and no one was social distancing. It was as if someone had asked them if they could demonstrate the exact opposite of it.

When it was my turn, I stayed back a few feet and

announced my name. The guy thrust his hand out to me and introduced himself as Nick. I looked down at his outstretched hand and said, "Nah, not really doing that anymore, but nice to meet you."

I heard him make a noise with his mouth. He withdrew his hand, saying, "Sorry, man. Force of habit. From my days of heading up a large corporation. Nice to meet you."

I laughed. Setting those "I'm the Boss" boundaries right off the mark.

"Same here, but I'd like to talk with you about something else before all this starts. Would you have a few minutes before the meeting?"

He looked at me and grimaced. "Not really, bud, just about to start this thing up, But I'm sure all of your questions will be answered by the end of my talk and the video, so just have a seat and we'll begin. I have a Q and A afterward, and we bring in pizza. We can talk then."

Video. I was in for the long haul. My ploy to get out of there early didn't work, but I felt I should get high marks for the attempt. Ah, the glamor of being a private investigator. Well, at least there was pizza.

I moved to the back of the room and stood against a wall, as far away from the next guy as possible, putting my mask up. No one else seemed to be concerned.

Nick called for attention, and the room quieted down. He walked everyone through the basics – how you get paid through direct deposit, how to download the app that signals each job and where the clients were, and how everyone would get a stipend to pay for cleaning the back seat if any kind of fluids were shed by the clients picked up. There was a palpable tension in the room when he said that. A young black woman raised her hand with a question.

"Does that happen often? I mean, I have a fairly new car. Do people bleed all over the back seat on a regular basis? I ain't having none of that."

It set everyone off. Nick put his hands up to calm the crowd.

"Listen, it's a rare occurrence for a client to bleed or urinate or defecate on your back seat but it does happen. What we are doing is providing you with the monies to have your car cleaned in the rare case that it does happen."

Three people and the black woman who asked the question got up and walked out, but the rest stayed. Jobs were still hard to come by. Nick continued.

"Okay, so we're gonna show a video right now that will hopefully answer all your questions, but if not, we'll have a Q&A afterwards when the pizza gets here."

A few hands shot up but he ignored them, cut the lights, and hit a switch on his computer. Video images flashed quickly and then the Veyo logo, followed by an announcer touting the joys of owning your own business that was different from the other ride-hailing companies. Everyone was waiting to hear the amounts each ride paid, but I took the opportunity to go find Nick and see if he knew anything. I could buy my own pizza.

He was sitting in a small office with the door open, going through the applications. There was another guy setting up a table with paper plates and plastic forks. I knocked on the outer wall to the office. I was aware the other guy was watching me, but I ignored him. Nick looked up at his desk, sighed, and said, "Can't it wait until the video is over?"

I gave him a hard look.

"Nick, I'm not really here for the job. I need to ask you some questions about one of your drivers. I'm looking for information about Earl Scosa. He's missing. Is there anything you can tell me about him?"

Nick squinted, deep in thought. "Who are you?"

"My name is Tommy Shore. I'm working for Earl's family. He disappeared over a week ago, and his last known job was working for you, for Veyo. I was hoping that you might know something. There's not a whole lot to go on, so I'm asking around in the last places he might have been seen."

I watched his face as he decided how much he wanted to be involved, looking at his watch a few times.

"Let's go outside. There still twenty minutes left on the video."

I followed him out of the office, up the stairs to the lot, and continued to follow him as he walked away from the doors. He looked around before talking to me, then said in a whispered voice, "There was definitely something wrong there."

I looked at him and could see he was afraid of something. I pressed him for more details.

"What do you mean?"

"Mr. Shore, Veyo is a great company that offers many benefits while helping those needing special attention. People do this job because, yes, they need the money, but also because they want to work for themselves. If you hustle, you could take down a hundred bucks an hour, but you really need to hustle. I mean, I never got the idea that Scosa was doing this job for real.

It felt to me like it was a way for him to drive around Wallingford and Meriden without raising any suspicions that he might be doing something else. When he first came to work with us, he seemed like a nice guy. I liked him. Quiet type, ya know? Worked hard in the beginning, made the pickups, put in a full day. But after a few weeks, he started taking fewer and fewer calls. I doubt that he made more than three or four pickups a day, but the tracker we use showed us that he was driving all over the place every day. Finally, he just stopped logging on."

I had been drifting slightly during the rah-rah part, but the last few sentences caught my attention.

"Say that again? You have the ability to track a driver's movements?"

He nodded. "Part of the function of the app is to track where a driver is, once they log on. We don't really tell drivers that because we've had some privacy issues in the past, but it's there. As long as the app is on and the phone is in the car, we can track movement."

"Do you archive any of that? Do you have a record of where a driver has been?"

Nick grimaced. "We only keep them going back for a week or two. Otherwise, the data would take up too much space in our system. I can take a look and see where the last spot he logged in from was."

He looked at his watch. "Listen, I gotta go back in and finish the seminar, but if you want to swing back here in an hour or so, say 6:30, we can take a look."

I thanked him, and he went back inside. I went back to the Chevy and sat for a few minutes. If he had information on where Scosa had been, it might give me a starting point toward where he might have been going.

I watched as a car pulled up and a guy got out with a half dozen pizzas. I thought about going in again to grab a slice or two but decided to find another place to eat. Besides, those people looked like they would make short work of whatever Nick ordered. Didn't want to irritate anyone any more than usual or get too close to people eating.

FIVE

I drove down route 5 toward Wallingford and the Connecticut Natural Food market, which was just over the North Haven line. It was a privately owned supermarket that had a terrific deli where they made killer sandwiches. During the lunch hours, the lines would be three people deep, typically construction guys or office workers or state road workers who worked at the transportation depot just off the highway there. However, at this hour, there would only be late grocery shoppers or people stopping in to pick up prepared foods for dinner that night.

I pulled into the lot and was surprised at the number of cars parked there. Hopefully, the market was getting new supplies. I would occasionally shop out there if people I knew were going and I could get a ride. I'd heard from those same friends that it had been touch-and-go, with the freezer cases nearly empty and the meat mostly gone, but they had stayed fully stocked with fresh vegetables and fruits and had kept their prices reasonable.

I parked, pulled my mask back out of my pocket, and went in. The line at the deli was short, but there were a few people ahead of me, so I took a number and waited. They used to have a small hot buffet with the special foods of the day, Mexican or wings and the like. But it was completely empty, with a sign telling shoppers to INQUIRE AT THE DELI COUNTER. The salad bar was likewise empty, so most of the folks getting dinner were over at the case with the prepared foods. When my number was called, I ordered a full steak and cheese sub with hot peppers, then crossed the store to grab a Foxon Park orange soda.

I took my time looking around. To the left of the cooler where the soft drinks were kept, I noticed a corkboard on the wall, where you could put up flyers looking for lost pets or advertise for someone to paint your house or clean your yard. One notice immediately caught my eye and gave me chills.

In the exact middle of the other notices, solidly held in place by a tack in each corner, was a typewritten piece of white paper:

IF YOU BELIEVE IN PURITY AND NATURAL SUPERI-ORITY AND ARE LOOKING FOR LIKE-MINDED BRETHREN, CALL THIS NUMBER TODAY. LEAVE A MESSAGE AND SOMEONE WILL GET BACK TO YOU.

Below that was a phone number and just below the number was the name KNIGHTS OF THE MESSAGE. It was the second time I'd heard mention of that name in the last two days. Remembering what Carla intimated about Earl, I took out my pad and jotted down the number.

I heard my ticket number being called and went back to the counter to pick up the bag with my sandwich in it. They always threw in a bag of kettle chips, and I took that out so the heat wouldn't make them soggy. At the register in front, the cashier had a mask on, but I could see she was very pretty, with eyes a beautiful pale blue. I smiled widely at her but then remembered my mask was on so it probably looked alarming to her. I paid and left to eat my dinner alone in my borrowed car.

The faux-Philly cheese steak was delicious, and while I tried to drag out the experience of it, I ended up finishing it quickly. I immediately wanted another but knew that another one, even half of one, would make me want a nap so I refrained from going back inside. Besides, the creepiness factor would be high if I had to pay for it with the same cashier.

I sipped the soda and looked over my notes again. Carla had mentioned that she had seen the word "purity" on one of the signs in the back seat of Earl's car. I put the pad down and picked up my phone, googling the Knights of The Message.

There wasn't much information, and most of what was there connected me to articles on the KKK. There were some *Hartford Courant* newspaper pieces written in the late 70s, and a few from the early 80s. One of the earlier ones was about a visit to the state that longtime Klan leader, Grand Wizard, and Holocaust denier David Duke made. He had toured Connecticut, Rhode Island and Massachusetts, evidently trying to drum up membership and sell his memorabilia. For 30 dollars, you could get a robe and a subscription to his newspaper, *The Crusade*. Quite the bargain.

The other articles were about a Klan rally in Meriden a year after Duke's tour. It was a dark moment in Connecticut history. After a Meriden cop shot a young black man for shoplifting at a nearby mall, the Klan had organized a support rally for the cop. It had turned violent when an anti-Klan group gathered to protest the rally, with dozens hurt and a number of arrests.

There was a smattering of shorter pieces written about the Klan in the area, most done in the late 8os. They all seemed to have concluded that the group had gone underground after those incidents. The only recent piece was from 2012 and tried to make the case that there were still factions at work in the area.

There was no mention of the Knights of The Message.

I finished eating my chips and downed my soda. My fingers were greasy from the mess of it all. I searched the glove box for napkins, but there were none there, so I walked back into the market. I made my way down to the rest rooms and grabbed some paper towels from the dispenser, being careful not to get too close to anyone as I left and trying not to get the attention of the cashier that had rung me out.

As I walked back across the parking lot and got closer to my car, I could see a large van had parked near me, with one space between the two vehicles. Written on the side of the van were the words CHRIS LYNDE – ELECTRICAL CONTRACTOR. The driver was standing on the passenger side of the van with his arms folded across his chest, watching me approach.

As I got closer, I could see he was about 5'9" or so and mostly thin, with a bit of a beer belly starting to show. Maybe in his late 40s, although he could have been older. It was difficult to tell. He was wearing a black Garth Brooks t-shirt, sleeves cut off to better show what I'm sure he thought were his bulging biceps, though there wasn't much to show. It was even more difficult to tell his age because of the MAGA hat he had on, sitting high atop his head, trucker style. He hadn't shaved in a few days, and the jeans and work boots that he had on were dirty, like he had recently done some manual labor. He had an unlit cigarette dangling from his lips to complete the image. He cleared his throat to stop me from getting into my car.

"I was at the Veyo meeting and followed you here. I waited to see what you were gonna do but decided we could talk here when I saw you go back inside. Figured you'd be out quick."

I looked closely at him, vaguely recognizing him as one of the guys who stood at the back of the wall, and tried to decide if he was friend or foe. I had yet to replace my sap that I'd lost to the police during my last case. Everything else I had to defend myself was back at the apartment. I thought I could possibly throw the handful of paper towels to distract him until I got in my car. I didn't think I'd need to, but I couldn't be sure if he had a weapon or not. I proceeded cautiously.

"What can I do for you, friend?"

He snorted. An actual snort.

"Not so much what you can do for me, *friend*, as much as what I can do for you. I followed you out of the meeting and overheard you talking to Nick. If you're looking for Earl Scosa, Nick's a dead end. He's afraid of his own shadow and wouldn't say shit if he had a mouthful."

I waited. I got the feeling he was building up to something.

"Me, on the other hand? I actually knew Earl. We started driving for Veyo at about the same time, signed up together and sat next to each other at the onboarding. Once we got to talking, we realized that we were both cut from the same cloth and got to be friends."

I wasn't sure where this was headed or how many more clichés he would use.

"And you are?" I wasn't sure if he worked for the company or was the owner.

He kept looking at me but narrowed his eyes. The thought that he had watched too many Clint Eastwood movies floated past me.

"Name's Chris but it don't matter who I am. What matters most is how bad do you want to find Earl?"

Ah, so this was a shakedown. I considered it for a second, not knowing if he could contribute anything and just how much I wanted to tell him. I decided to appeal to his humanity.

"I'm working for Earl's sister-in-law, who's taking care of Earl's little girl. She and her husband are working people who don't have much money. He disappeared a week ago and she asked me to try and find out where he went or if something happened. I started with Veyo because that's the last place Earl worked. If you know something, I'd like to hear it."

He looked at me, a weird smirk on his face.

"How much is the information worth to you?"

So much for humanity. I looked him in the eyes until he turned away.

"Depends on the information you have. A warning, though, if I hear it and it's not really worth anything,

I'm definitely going to give your name to the Walling-ford police. Once this is an official manhunt, they'll be looking for all parties of interest, and that would definitely include you."

The smirk left his face.

"You wouldn't do that. Besides, you don't know my full name."

His level of stupidity made me laugh, and I made a show of turning my head toward the lettering on his van. He followed my gaze and I could see him swallow hard.

"I'm pretty sure I do. Look, tell me what you know, then we both get in our vehicles and leave, no harm done. I'll even mention that you helped me if anything comes of it. Okay?"

I watched as he considered the offer, looking at the ground. When he looked up, he seemed ready to talk.

"Okay. Well, like I said, me and Earl were friends. I was doing this at first for the extra cash but I kept driving through this whole virus thing because a lot of folks were staying home and nobody wanted to let an electrician in. Even the ones who kept using Veyo were only doing it to get to the methadone clinics. There was a lot less work, so Earl and I would meet up sometimes for lunch at a local barbecue place in town or go for a beer after we were done driving. We'd bullshit or talk about the clients that we picked up during the day. Some of 'em were real beauties, good for a laugh. Like, one guy..."

I put up my hand to stop him. "Save the war stories, Chris. All I need is anything you think would be helpful. Whatever it was you were gonna sell me." I added a sneer at the end of that to indicate I still thought he was a scumbag for even approaching me with it. He got the gist.

"Okay, okay. I get it. Earl started getting involved with this group in town. A lot of times I'd check in with him to see if he wanted to meet up, but lots of times he couldn't talk or wouldn't even answer his cell. Later, when we'd meet up, he'd say he had been busy running personal errands. Honestly, I thought he had a little something on the side, if you know what I mean, and that he was stopping in to see her. Didn't really need to be secret about it, his wife had been killed years ago. After a while, my curiosity got the better of me, and I asked him point blank what the deal was. We were eating in our cars, you know, cooping like the cops do, window to window, when I asked him what was going on, and he told me about this group that he was getting involved in. They would hold meetings in a local Elks club basement here every two or three weeks, always at different times. He said as the new guy, he was supposed to let members know when the meetings were. I guess they wanted it kept secret because they wouldn't use the phones or email to do it. It had to be in person. Earl was in his car all day, so I guess it just worked out that he could do it."

I considered what he was telling me. It certainly jibed with the signs in the back of Earl's car that Carla saw, but it went completely against the kind of guy she said he was. Or at least the way he used to be. She said he'd changed a lot since his wife died, but this seemed like a lot. I pushed Chris for more.

"So, you think he was involved with one of these groups and that something happened? Did he give you any indication that there was trouble, that something could go wrong?"

Chris shook his head. "Earl didn't say anything, but I've lived and worked in this area my whole life. There's a lot of shady characters around. Lots of bad guys who haven't been happy with the way the town changed over the last twenty, thirty years. You know, minorities and the like."

I nodded, then looked at my phone and saw that it was close to when I needed to head back to Veyo and see what Nick might have.

"Look, this has been a help. I might need some more information from you, but I need to leave now. It's possible there could be something in it for you. I know how to contact you from the number on the van. Would you be willing to talk again if needed?"

He jerked his head back a little, surprised at how this had turned around.

"Yeah, sure, you can always call me. I can help you maneuver around the town. Like I said, I know a lot of people and about the stuff that goes on."

I said thanks and got in my car, jotting down his number from the van before he got in and left, giving me a little wave as he pulled a U-turn and sped out of the lot. Everybody loves intrigue. I laughed and headed back to North Haven and Veyo.

SIX

Pulling back into the driveway of Veyo's at exactly 6:30, I knew immediately that something was off. There wasn't a single car in the lot, and unless Nick lived within walking distance, he'd already left. I pulled into a spot near the doors, got out, and tried them. They were both locked.

Remembering that Nick had been taking calls on his cell, I looked back at the email confirmation I'd received for the meeting, trying to find a phone number I could call. I found it and called but there was no answer.

Not sure what to do next, I got in the car and drove back home.

Once I was back inside my apartment, I took out the ancient laptop and googled Veyo again, looking for any possible way to contact Nick. Most of the material was online reviews. They ranged from just okay to mediocre, with an occasional 4-star thrown in. There were a few ads for joining up, but the number listed to call was the same as the one I had. I kept scrolling down until I lit upon a small article about the company when it first started in Connecticut. They'd evidently had some trouble at first getting the permits they needed but were eventually granted permission to operate in the state and allowed to tie in to Medicaid. The article said the permittee was one Nicholas Varsha.

There was another number listed for him when I googled his name and I called it immediately. After five rings, a woman answered in a sleepy voice. I looked at my phone and saw it was just before 9:00—a bit early for bed, unless she works a weird shift.

"Hi, this is Tommy Shore. I'm looking for Nick Varsha, is this the right number?"

I heard a yawn, then, "Nick's not here. At meeting. Try cell phone," followed by another yawn. There was an Eastern European tinge to her voice, Ukrainian or Czech. Maybe she was a vampire.

"But I do have the right number, yes? Nick does live there, the guy who runs drivers for Veyo?"

There was nothing for thirty seconds, then, "Yes, Veyo. Try the cell," and then a click followed by a dial tone. I called Nick's cell again and got his voice mail. I left a message that I'd try again tomorrow.

I called Carla, and Shana answered. She sounded excited and repeated what her aunt had evidently taught her to say.

"Hi, Shana. This is Tommy. I was at your house the other day. Kinda late, isn't it? Don't you have to go to school tomorrow?"

She laughed, called me silly again, and told me there was no school, it was "'cation" but that her aunt was teaching her on the internet with her teacher and other kids on Zoom. I shook my head at yet another weird change in the world.

"Oh, I get it now. Thanks for clearing that up. Do you mind if I speak to your Aunt Carla then?"

I heard a squeal, followed by the sound of the receiver hitting a wall. In the background I could hear her yelling, and a few seconds later Carla came on.

"Yes, Mr. Shore. This is Carla. Sorry about Shana, but we're teaching her to use the phone. I hope she wasn't rude."

I laughed. "Not at all, a perfect little lady. Listen, I just wanted to touch base. I started asking around about Earl, and there's a bunch of loose ends that I'm chasing. There's nothing much to report as this point, but I wanted to let you know what I've been doing."

She hesitated before she said, "So, does this mean that you're taking the case, that you'll help us?"

I considered my approach. "Well, it means that there seems to be more to this than it looks on the surface, and I'm intrigued. So, I'm gonna spend another day or two digging into it before I start the clock on you paying me. Is that okay?"

Another hesitation. "Mr. Shore, I do appreciate it. I want to be clear that I'm not asking you to do this as a favor, that I fully intend to pay you. If I can't handle it all up front, I can maybe do it over time? Would that work for you?"

I wanted to put her at ease but realized she was a very proud person. "Carla, I completely understand and will definitely charge you for my services. I just want to make sure that there's more to this than just a runaway dad. If it helps, I can take a few hundred upfront for expenses. I can swing by at the end of the week."

That seemed to do the trick, and we agreed that I would call her before I came to the house, then hung up. I went to the fridge for something to drink but ended up taking a pint of Häagen-Dazs Coffee Almond Crunch out and finishing the remaining half.

I spent a little more time online, trying to find out more information about fringe groups and about Wallingford. There wasn't much more there than what I had already seen, but I found an article that ran in the *Record Journal*, a small local paper that covered Meriden, Wallingford, and a few more surrounding towns. In it, the reporter, Renee Costa, seemed to be investigating some of the fringe groups that had been popping up in the area over the last few years. What surprised me was that this article was dated 2018. Her contention was that, not only were these groups still in existence, they were going strong. I looked her up to see whether she was still working for the paper, and she still had a byline. There was no follow-up I could find. I closed the laptop and made a mental note that I would go out to Wallingford tomorrow to see if I could speak to someone in the police department, then go and try to see Ms. Costa at the newspaper. If she was still there.

I made one more phone call, dialing up Rosalind, the nurse I had been dating for a while. It had been months since I'd last seen her. She had been called in to work every day as an "essential" person in the Yale-New Haven hospital ER but had decided that she wanted to be with her daughter in California during the quarantine, getting one of the last flights out before the airlines cut much of the service to many locations. She had been out there ever since.

She picked up after a few rings.

"Mr. Shore! So nice to hear from you. I was beginning to think you fell off the face of the earth!"

I laughed.

"Hey, I'm not the one across the country. How goes it out there?"

She laughed. I loved her laugh.

"Just dandy. All good. Suzanne and I are having the best time. We cook, grocery shop, cook, sit on the deck and drink, cook, drive around...did I mention we cook?"

"You did. Several times. Is she doing okay?"

Her daughter Suzanne had been on the front lines of the pandemic, working multiple shifts as both the fire safety coordinator for Santa Monica and doing double duty as dispatch for the fire department. Rosalind told me it got intense for a while and that Suzanne was beginning to think having her mother out there to come home to each night was a godsend.

"She's doing great. Busy, but she's back on a regular schedule. We're both waiting for when we can go to the bars and restaurants and meet up with her friends. They're saying it'll be any day now. Hopefully soon. I have a return ticket for mid-August and will probably go back on shifts at the hospital in early September. I miss my house! All my stuff is there! But enough about me, what's up with you? Getting outside for a little sunshine, now that you can?"

I smiled. She was always concerned about my health.

"I am. Gotta new case, in Wallingford, missing person. Not much to go on but these folks really need the help. It's kind of a tough situation. Not sure what I can do, but I'm gonna try and get them some answers."

I heard her chuckle. "Ah yes, the White Knight rides again. I love that about you. Well, be careful. Lots of crazies out there."

If she only knew the half of it.

We made some more small talk and promised to touch base again in a few days. I asked her to send my best to Suzanne, and we hung up.

I laid back and thought about the phrase she used, off the cuff, about the "White Knight." The irony of it wasn't lost on me.

I started to doze, with bits of the conversation running around in my brain until I came to the part about missing her house. It occurred to me that Carla might have a key to where Earl and Shana lived and that I needed to go there. It might turn up nothing, but it was worth a shot.

I put it on tomorrow's mental to-do list and tried to get some sleep.

SEVEN

The next morning, I awoke around 8:00, groggy and cranky. It had been a difficult night, with falling asleep almost impossible as my brain kept nagging at something unidentifiable. When I finally dozed, I was awakened by a dream that intruders had broken in to my apartment, dressed in sheets and hoods, trying to push me out of bed to get the sheets I was sleeping on. Half asleep, I pulled the mattress sheet off, and both pillows were on the floor. I got up, grabbed a pillow, and made my way to the couch, until I finally went to sleep.

I put together a pot of strong coffee in the French press and took a shower while it steeped, going over the list in my head as the hot water pounded my neck. Going to Scosa's place would be first on my agenda.

I dressed, got the car, and headed out of the garage toward Wallingford on I-95. I called Carla to tell her I was on my way, and she asked that I give her an hour, so I was taking my time. I was still trying to shake the cobwebs when I started noticing the billboards on the highway. They were religious, with phrases like "What is Truth? I Am Truth" next to a picture of Jesus, and "In the Beginning, God Created," with a phone number to call. I had never noticed them before, but I hadn't spent much time in this part of the state. It may have been my mental state, but they gave me a weird feeling.

When I got to Carla's, her car was in the driveway, but there was a van parked behind it. I could make out the faded words, "Vitter Lock and Safe" on the side where someone had tried to erase them without having to repaint the van. Evidently her husband, Paul, was home. I parked in front and went up the stairs to the porch.

Paul answered when I rang, opening the inside door but leaving the screen door closed.

"Yes?"

I wasn't sure if he knew about me so I proceeded cautiously.

"Good morning, Sir. Name's Tommy Shore. Your wife asked me to look into the disappearance of your brother-in-law, Earl. I called and she's expecting me."

He pushed open the screen door and moved sideways to indicate I was to enter.

"Paul, Carla's husband. Have a seat, she'll be out in a few. Puttin' on war paint."

He was a slight man, but my first impression was that he was wiry like a boxer on the lower end of the welterweight class, maybe 160 pounds. He also seemed quite a bit older than Carla, early 60s or so, but it might have been the ruddiness of his face that made me think that. I recognized the signs of alcohol abuse. The capillaries in his nose were broken, along with a splotchy redness on his jawline and neck. His nose had also been broken once or twice. He had a full head of dirty blonde hair that looked brittle, as if he had washed it too many times.

I sat down on the couch where Shana had been the last time I was here, doing her puzzle. The puzzle was still there. Paul sat in a rocking chair that was close to the front door.

"So, Carla said she saw your ad and called you, asked you to look into finding Earl. Didn't give you any cash, though."

It was a statement to show me he knew what was going on.

I nodded but didn't answer. He continued.

"Well, if you ask me, I think you're gonna find that Earl just plain took off. Carla says he wasn't that type, but I don't agree. He knew Carla loved that little girl and that we'd take care of her if he left. I've seen his kind before. All kinds of righteous upfront, but the minute the going gets tough, they're out of there. Worked with people like that all my life. Can't trust 'em as far as you can throw 'em. And that ain't far, ya know what I mean?"

I continued nodding. I got the feeling I wasn't actually required to say anything.

"You a drinker, Mr. Shore? I used to be. Hard core. Been working the program for five years and two months. Saved my marriage and definitely saved my life."

Guess it was my turn as he looked like he was waiting for a response.

"Please call me Tommy. Yes, I like a drink every now and again. Why do you ask?"

He narrowed his eyes at me. "Because I don't trust anybody who drinks to excess. And I wouldn't want that kind of person around my niece, either. I've seen lots of bad behavior over the years, Tommy, and all of it can be sourced back to drinking or drugs. You use drugs?"

This was becoming a very weird conversation with someone I had just met. I'd known my share of reformed alkies, and a lot of them make sobriety the center of their lives. This felt like an audition. I started to answer him when Carla came into the room.

I could tell she had been crying. Her eyes were puffy, even though the makeup she had applied didn't cover it up and her skin was splotchy. Her hands were shaking slightly, and she wouldn't look directly at me.

"Good morning, Mr. Shore. I see you got a chance to meet my husband, Paul."

I started to answer but Paul interrupted.

"Yeah, we were just getting to know one another. I was just asking him some questions about his habits."

I saw her blush. She tried to change the subject.

"Can I get you anything, Mr. Shore? Coffee or tea? Maybe a soft drink?"

Once again, before I could answer, Paul chimed in. His voice was filled with annoyance.

"He don't need nuthin' to drink. He just wants his cash. Am I right, *Tom*?"

He spit out the shortened version of my name like he thought it was inappropriate that a grown man should be called Tommy. I'd seen this kind of bully before. We locked eyes and I could tell he was looking for a fight. I wasn't going to engage. I stood up and spoke directly to Carla.

"No, thank you, Carla. Kind of you to offer but I want to get a jump on things. You said you had a spare key to Earl's apartment? If I could get that, I can take a look around and see if there's anything there that might be useful."

Carla turned to get the key from a nail that hung just inside the kitchen door. It was on a key ring that had a small facsimile of a Connecticut State Police badge on it. She handed it to me, along with a piece of paper with the address on it. I looked at the key ring and then up at Carla.

"You said Earl flunked out of the state police academy, right? He must have wanted it pretty badly if he bought all the keepsakes."

Carla started to answer, but Paul jumped in again.

"Flunked out? That guy couldn't keep a job if his life depended on it. He musta tried a dozen of them. This last one, chauffeuring drug addicts around on the state's teat, was a perfect job for him, sitting on his butt all day and driving them to pick up their methadone. And who pays for that? We do, with our taxes. Don't get me started!"

I was about to say something back to him when I looked at Carla and saw the level of embarrassment this was causing her. I decided to stick to my plan of not engaging and turned toward her, with my back to him.

"I'm going to take a look around their place, but it shouldn't take me long. Will there be any issues from the neighbors or a building manager, a doorman, or security maybe?"

Paul snorted. "There ain't none of that over there. Lucky the door locks work at all. Not the best part of town, if you know what I mean? Let's just say Earl didn't have to drive far to make his pickups."

He snorted again. I turned from Carla and went out

the front door as quickly as I could, not sure how long I could keep from saying something. I was down the steps when I heard the screen door open and close, with Carla coming down the stairs.

"Mr. Shore, Tommy...I'm sorry. He's just in a mood. I hadn't told him about you until this morning, and he didn't take to it much. Here."

She reached into her apron and pulled out money that had been folded over, with a 20-dollar bill on top, held together with a small, yellow paper clip. She extended the packet out to me. There were five 20s all together.

"I know it's not a lot but it might help a little with your expenses, gas and food and such. Please take it, Tommy. I promise, you will get paid for this job. As soon as..."

I stopped her. "Carla, the last thing you need to worry about right now is me. You have your hands full with Shana and everything else."

I glanced at the doorway. Paul had gotten up and was standing there again. I made a show of taking the cash and putting in my pocket, raising my voice so he could hear me.

"As soon as I find out anything, I'll call you...or maybe I'll just show up and see if you're home. Either way, I'll be in touch soon."

I got in my car, pulled into the next driveway, turned around, and then headed back the way I came. I could see her watching me as I drove off and him still in the doorway. I refrained from waving.

EIGHT

Heading toward the police department, I tried to control my anger through a deep breathing technique that a friend had shown me, but it wasn't really helping. I was still pissed, and now I was lightheaded to boot.

The Wallingford police department was located on North Main Street, away from the restaurants and businesses that made up most of the street. From what I found online, it held the offices of key personnel, the detective division, the traffic division, dispatch, and all of the records from accident reports to criminal histories. When I entered the building, I expected to find a fair amount of hustle and bustle, given all that went on there, but there was only one older woman sitting at a desk behind a partition, answering phones. I walked over to her and waited for her to get off her call. When she did, she busied herself with some paperwork and then, after a minute or so, looked at me, peering over her glasses.

"Yes, can I help you?"

I handed her my card.

"Hi. My name is Tommy Shore. I'm an investigator who's been retained by a family that lives here in Wallingford to look into the disappearance of one of their family members. I was hoping there'd be someone of weight I could talk to?"

She looked up from my card, and her eyebrows arched as she shook her head indicating she didn't understand what I meant.

"Of weight?"

"My apologies. Someone who's in charge, perhaps the chief or one of the lead detectives?"

She looked at me, deciding how to handle this, then said, "Please hold," and pressed a button on her phone. I heard it ring a few times until someone answered. She looked at me while she spoke to whoever was on the other end.

"Hi, it's Julie. Is Jack or Ron around? There's a gentleman out here who would like to speak with a detective. He's a private investigator, says he's working on finding a missing person, someone from town."

The other person said something, and Julie laughed, then said she'd wait. Thirty seconds later, she said "Okay" to the other person and hung up. She looked at me and smiled.

"Ron Decker is one of the detectives here and has agreed to see you. Please have a seat. He'll come out and get you as soon as he's free."

She motioned toward three small chairs that were over by a wall, under a plaque commemorating the department for its fund-raising efforts on behalf of the Wallingford Little League. There was a small table between the first chair and the next two, with a box of Kleenex on it and a pump bottle of hand sanitizer, almost gone. Doing their part in the ongoing battle against the virus. There were no magazines or brochures, nothing that could possibly be a conductor. I looked at my phone for messages, but there was only one missed call that left a message about lowering my credit card rates.

After five minutes or so, a man came down the hall toward me.

Decker looked to be about 45 or 50 years old but had clearly started losing his hair early in life and now wore it in a close-cropped ring above his ears. He was a good thirty pounds overweight, centered all in his belly, which hung over his belt. He wore a dark tie that was pulled down at the neck, giving the impression that he had been working hard, with the sleeves of his rumpled white shirt rolled up to the crook of his elbow. He had cold eyes and a prominent nose, beneath which was a dark mustache. It was unkempt and moved around on his face as he seemed to be finishing the chewing of either a late breakfast or an early lunch. He stopped about five feet from me.

"Shore?"

I was the only one in the lobby. I immediately saw how he made detective.

"That's me. Friends call me Tommy."

He nodded, then waved me to come back to his office. Evidently, he had enough friends.

His office was at the end of the hall, opposite the precinct captain's, which was dark. I followed him, and he motioned for me to sit as he sat down. There were two wooden, straight-backed chairs in front of his desk. I took the one closest to the window, which was open. The old building seemed to have central air conditioning, but it wasn't flowing into this office very well. On his desk were the remains of a BLT, and the smell of that, along with sweat and something indeterminable, hung in the air. Decker wrapped up the remainder of the sandwich and put it in a drawer, then took a final swig from a bottle of Yoo-hoo he'd been drinking and tossed that into a waste bucket near the wall, basketball style. He made the shot, gave a small pump of his arm, and then turned toward me.

"What can I do for you, Tom?"

I got the sense from his tone that he was just going through the motions, humoring me. I gave him one of my cards.

"I'm a private investigator. I've been hired by a woman who lives here in town, Carla Vitter. She asked me to look into the disappearance of her brother-in-law, who's been missing for over a week. She said she called here a couple of times but hit a dead end. I was hoping you might be able to fill me in on what your department is doing about it."

I tried to say it as unaggressively as I could, but I could see from the change in his demeanor that he took it as an affront.

"We haven't done a god-damn thing about it. As far as we're concerned, there isn't even a viable complaint yet. Guys take off all the time, leaving their family in the lurch when it gets too heavy. We have no reason to think that there's anything else going on here. Unless, of course, you uncovered a big fat clue that'll makes us reconsider?"

His reaction confirmed that they had at least looked at the complaint and that something else was at play here. Carla said she'd been told the police wouldn't get involved because they were too busy with virus-related stuff, but this made me think they had dismissed it out of hand, for whatever reason.

"I was just curious as to why no one has even gone over to her house and taken a report? It's a missing person's complaint in your town, and that would be the least that could be done. Doesn't it merit an investigation, even a low priority one?"

Decker sighed, reached in to a drawer, and pulled out a yellow legal pad, throwing it on his desk so it made a noise, and then grabbed a pen out of a Yankees mug that sat on the desk close to me.

"Okay, give me the names again and the address, and we'll send someone over to check it out."

I gave him the information, and he wrote it down, then stood and said, "I have your card. We'll be in touch."

It was clear I was being dismissed, so I left his office. I could hear the sandwich paper rustling as he took the remainder of what he'd been eating out of the drawer. It reminded me that I hadn't eaten yet today. I was pissed off and needed something tasty to tamp down the anger.

I'd read that Wallingford was famous for steamed cheeseburgers and made a mental note that I'd try one. I stopped back at the receptionist's desk to ask her if she knew a good place close by that served them. She was talking quietly to a uniformed cop but stopped when I approached.

"Hello again, I'm not from here. Do either of you know where the best place to get a steamed cheeseburger would be?"

They looked at each and the cop said, "Probably Woody's, near the train station. There's a couple of famous places up in Meriden, Ted's and K LaMay's, but I like the ones we have here."

The receptionist nodded in agreement, and the cop gave me directions. It was close by.

I thanked them both and walked out. I would see him again, sooner than I liked.

NINE

I drove out of the police station and headed back toward Center Street, then down the hill and across Route 5 to the train station.

The Wallingford train station was a small stop on the train lines that ran between Hartford and New Haven. It was serviced by Amtrak and the CT Hartford lines. The original station had been built in the late 1800s and was designated as a historic building. The newer station, a small building with parking, was built and started operating in 2016. I pulled into that lot, parked, and then crossed the street to Woody's.

There was a small counter with only six stools. It was still early, and the lunch crowd, whatever that might look like, hadn't come in yet. They were letting people inside, so I sat at the stool closest to the door.

The cook sat behind the counter at the other end, reading a newspaper. He looked up when I walked in but quickly went back to his paper. He looked like Mel from that old TV show about the diner, right down to his t-shirt and apron. I read the chalk board menu above the back counter, which held a variety of bottles with pumps, evidently flavors for making sodas from scratch. A good sign.

To the left of the counter was a large copper box, with a tray of water beneath it, simmering. There looked to be twenty or so small drawers that made up the top part of the box. I'd never seen anything like it in a restaurant.

After a minute or two, the owner closed his paper and came down toward my end, grabbing a napkin/fork setup from under the counter and putting it down in front of me.

"How many ya want?"

I must have looked confused because the next thing he asked was, "First time?"

I nodded and said, "Walk me through it?"

He chuckled. "Wow. A newbie. Hardly see that much anymore. Sure. Well, that box over there cooks the burgers using steam and melts the cheese in these little drawers...kinda like a burger hotel. Gives it a different taste. We serve it on a bulkie roll. Holds up better. And we make all of our drinks from scratch: seltzer and you pick the flavoring. Lemon/lime is our bestseller. Start with one, and if you want more, I'll get ya another one. I'm Chip."

"Woody out today?"

He laughed, a big hearty laugh. I liked him.

"Nah, it's my joint. I called it Woody's because I'm a big "Cheers" fan, and it sounded good. Besides, there was already a crappy place called "CHIPS" in Southington."

"Okay then, well, I'm gonna take your recommendation and get one burger and the lemon/lime soda."

He nodded and turned to grab a roll and started making my burger. He placed it in front of me in under two minutes, then turned to make the soda. I dug in and was immediately struck by the texture and the saltiness. It was a little weird. Without being cooked in butter or oil, it tasted watery to me. Not necessarily bad, just weird. The soda was refreshing, though, and I downed that, leaving a quarter of the burger uneaten. Unusual for me but it felt like it was a microcosm of the town itself, a little off-kilter. I threw ten bucks on the counter and left.

Once back in the car, I decided to take another shot at the Veyo place, opting to follow Route 5 through Wallingford down into North Haven. It was much the same on the main thoroughfare as it was in town--car dealerships, old stores selling keepsakes or vacuum cleaners, small mom-and-pop restaurants that looked dark and might never reopen, a Dairy Queen with one masked person at the window, an enormous CVS, and some large factories just across the train tracks. Everytown, USA.

I just passed the market where I'd bought the cheesesteak and was stopped for a light when I was saw there was a police cruiser behind me. As the light changed, the cruiser lit up and flashed for me to pull over. I turned right at the light, went over the tracks, and pulled in the parking lot of a wholesale flooring company.

I took out my wallet and reached over to the glovebox for the registration, but when I looked in the rearview mirror, I could see the cop wasn't getting out of his car. I wasn't sure what to do, so I waited.

A good ten minutes went by before I saw his door

open, and he approached my car. Even though he was wearing a Covid-19 mask, I recognized him as the cop who gave me the steamed cheeseburger advice. I lowered the window and was waiting for instructions, but he stood about four feet from the car and didn't say a word for a good 30 seconds. It confused me. He pulled down his mask.

"Do you want my license and registration?" I asked.

He shook his head and just kept looking at me. His badge indicated his name was Rich.

"Well, is this where I ask what's this all about?"

Always a good idea to quote Chandler.

He smiled but still didn't answer. I tried again.

"Is Rich your first name or last name?"

There was no discernible reaction but he finally spoke.

"Yeah, Decker said you were a wise guy. I find most people turn to humor when they're at their most scared. Are you scared, Mr. Shore?"

I ran through it in my head quickly. He had spoken to Decker, he knew my name, and he had pulled me over for no apparent reason. I shook my head and let him talk.

"Well, you should be. You're messing around with people that don't like intruders. Call this a warning, Mr. Shore. Drop this thing you're looking into. It will get you hurt. That's a promise. Have a nice day."

He walked back to his cruiser, got in, pulled a sharp U-turn out of the lot, and then sped back toward the center of town.

I sat there, trying to figure out what the hell just happened. After a couple of minutes, I scrapped going to Veyo, got on the highway, and headed toward the Trinity.

Traffic had definitely started to increase again, and it took me a while to get downtown. I found a space close to the bar's entrance and went in. Michael was working the bar. I hoped Lindsay would be on, as I didn't feel like running through the whole "Whad'ya been up to" tap dance again. I liked Michael a lot, but he was pure Irish, and the gift of gab was strong in him.

"Tommy boy, great to see ya, what's the good word? Ya look like hell. How about a Jameson?"

I smiled, nodded, and waited, but he poured my drink, put it in front of me, and then went down the bar to wait on another customer. He must have been tired of the small talk, too.

I looked at my phone and saw that I'd missed two calls, one from Carla and the other from an unknown number. Both had left messages. I picked up the one from the unknown caller first.

"Mr. Shore, Nick from Veyo. Sorry about the other night. I couldn't wait. Felt like someone had been watching us, and I didn't want to hang around by myself after everyone left. Hope you understand. Tanya told me you called the house. Please don't do that again, use my cell? Thanks. Anyway, please call me and we can set up a meeting time to look at the system regarding Earl Scosa. Take care."

Looking through my notes, I found what I had written down about Nick and Veyo. He had said they only archived the log-ons going back a week or two. I needed to see him quickly if I wanted to pinpoint where Earl might have been when he disappeared. I hit "redial" and he picked up after two rings.

"Mr. Shore. Thanks for calling back. Sorry about the other night."

"No worries, Nick. Thank you for reaching out. Are you at the Veyo office?"

He told me that he was on his way there now and that I could come meet him. I agreed and hung up.

Michael came back down to ask me if I wanted lunch. I shook my head and told him about the steamed cheeseburger in Wallingford and how it was just sitting in my gut. He picked up the mixer gun and pulled a tall glass of club soda, telling me to drink it down in one gulp. I did as I was told and belched appreciatively. It actually felt better. I threw a 10 on the bar and left, headed back to North Haven.

TEN

There were cars in the lot, but I found a space and went in the door that led downstairs. It was dark in the stairwell and hallway, but I could see a light down where the Veyo meeting had been and could hear noises, like stuff being thrown around. I had nothing on me for protection and kicked myself for putting off replacing my sap, making a mental note to do so as soon as I got back to my apartment.

Proceeding cautiously, I came to where Nick's small office was. He was on his knees with his back to me, putting files back into folders that had evidently been thrown around the room. The drawers to the small cabinet they came from were all open, and everything else in the room was askew, as if someone had rifled through the place quickly. The table that the Mr. Coffee had been on was pulled away from the wall, and the entire unit was laying on its side, the glass pot in pieces on the floor. Papers were strewn all over the floor. Empty pizza boxes stacked for recycling had been tossed around and the two wastebaskets that held used cups were overturned. Many of them had held varying levels of liquid, coffee, or soft drinks, and that had spilled out, perfuming the air with a sickly-sweet stench.

I cleared my throat softly to let him know I was there, but he still jumped from the surprise. When he saw it was me, he grimaced and pointed his finger at me.

He said, "This is your fault" and kept trying to gather up the paperwork.

There was an overturned chair near me, so I righted it and sat down.

"How so?"

"How so? The goons who did this must have found out I was going to show the stuff you wanted to see and sent someone here to warn me not to. I can't think of another reason."

He was working hard to keep his voice under control, but it was obvious he was extremely upset. I kept my voice neutral.

"No way it could be an unhappy driver or a pissed off creditor?"

He stopped working and looked at me like I had two heads.

"Really? Really? No, this wasn't a driver or a bill collector. This is somebody trying to tell me not to help you," then went back to gathering paperwork.

I shook my head. "And how did they know that you were helping me? I haven't told anyone. Have you? I doubt it. So, is the place bugged? I doubt that, too. Is your cell being tapped? No, no one would go through that kind of hassle and expense. I think this was one of your guys who overheard us talking, or saw us, put it together, then went to someone else with the information. This looks half-assed, and I agree: whoever did this wasn't looking for something, they were sending a message. This is clumsy, strong-arm shit."

He looked at me with shock on his face. "Who? Who saw us? Who would sell me out like that?"

"Chris Lynde. He braced me after we talked the first time the other night. Thought he could make a quick buck, but I dissuaded him from that notion. He's not that bright, and I don't think he necessarily sold you out, just that he has a big mouth and probably let it slip about what he saw and what he thought it was about. It got back to the wrong guys, and they wanted to nip it in the bud. That's what this is."

Nick got angry again. "I can't have this, Mr. Shore. I run a legitimate business that has ties to state funding, and I can't have this kind of bad publicity getting out. They could screw with my charter and cause me a lot of grief. And I can't have them poking around in my personal business, either. I'd like you to leave."

I thought back to the sleepy lady who answered his home phone and wondered if she was here illegally. If that was the case, having someone in his business would be bad. I took one last shot.

"Listen all I need is to know the last location that Earl Scosa logged in from. I get that, I'm gone. You never see me again. I need a lead and, soft as this one is, it's the only one out there. If not for me, do it for a little girl who has to come to terms that her daddy isn't coming home any longer."

I cringed to myself as soon as I said it, but I needed the information, and I was losing the fight to get it.

He looked at me for a good 30 seconds, then

unlocked the door to his small office and hit the button to turn the computer on. After logging in, he typed in a bunch of stuff, then stared at the screen until he finally said, "1 1 0 North Plains Industrial Road. That's the last place he logged in from. Now, can I get back to putting this place together? I have a meeting this afternoon."

I thanked him and walked out.

Leaving North Haven, I decided to go to Earl's apartment first and see if anything revealed itself to me. After that, I would find the address Nick just gave me and see if that led anywhere. I wasn't hopeful. Nothing seemed to be panning out so far, and it all felt like grasping at straws. I called Carla from the car but got her machine and left a message to call me later that night.

Earl's apartment was in another nondescript building on a road that ran parallel to Route 5. It had been shoved in between a bevy of office buildings that made up much of the area and shared a driveway with an office building that housed a large insurance company. I pulled in and drove around to the back, parking in one of the back spaces that let me watch the entrance. There were no other cars parked there that seemed to belong to the apartment building. The tenants were probably blue collar, working people, back to their jobs after the long layoff.

No one went in or out of that entrance during the fifteen minutes I sat there, so I got out and walked over. There were no video cameras that I could see, and I was relieved to find that there was no security swipe lock on the door. Most likely cost cutting during construction.

Once inside, I waited a minute until my eyes

adjusted, then went up a dark staircase to the third floor. 110G was in the middle of the floor, and I moved down the hall quickly. I had been worried about neighbors, but no one seemed to be at home. The key Carla gave me fit in to the lock on the door handle easily, and I was inside in less than 10 seconds. I found the switch near the door and flipped on the lights. Looking around, I could see a life in complete disarray.

It was a tiny place, with a small kitchenette to the right, a half-wall separating it from the living room. An older television on a stand, a beat-up loveseat, and a straight back chair made up most of the living room. In front of the loveseat was a makeshift coffee table, a plank of plywood resting on two plastic milk crates, and next to the loveseat was a shelving unit that held various knickknacks and framed pictures of Earl and Janet when she was still pregnant with Shana. Happier times.

There were toys everywhere, as well as clothes and fast food containers, empty pizza boxes, and french-fry cartons. On the table were empty beer bottles and soda cans, maybe a half dozen, along with bills and other paperwork. I looked through the paperwork quickly. It seemed to be mostly dunning letters or subscription come-ons.

There was a sharp odor in the air, and the heat of the day wasn't helping. I found another switch in the kitchenette and flipped it on. A small overhead fan began to rotate. It didn't help much, but it moved the air around.

I went through the other door leading to the back of the apartment, and it was much the same. I turned on the overhead light to reveal a tiny bedroom. To the immediate left, there was a five-drawer bureau with a mirror sitting on top of it. Below the mirror was a small extra drawer for jewelry. Against a back wall, there was a twin bed that was unmade and, on the floor next to it, a small sleeping bag where Shana evidently slept.

I went through the five drawers but found nothing until the bottom drawer, where a small tin lockbox was hiding under some t-shirts. The box had seen better days and had a small dent on the top, like someone had hit it with their fist. The lock had a tiny key on a string stuck in it. I opened the box and looked through it. There were some insurance policies and a deed to a piece of property, along with various other documents. I grabbed the entire bundle and tucked it into my pants, between my belt and my back, then put the box back. I'd go through it later. The other drawers were empty.

I looked around again quickly and moved into the bathroom off the bedroom. It was barely big enough for one person, and I wondered how three people existed in the apartment. There were no clues, but I learned the source of the rank smell. There was a hamper and when I opened it, I gagged from the mix of body odor and gasoline, all coming from a work shirt that evidently had been in there awhile. I closed the lid quickly.

Back out in the kitchenette, I looked through the built-in drawers next to the stove. There were the usual silverware and cooking utensils in the top two drawers, but the bottom drawer contained more paperwork, held together with a wide elastic band. I flipped through the stack quickly but didn't have time to go through it all carefully. I was already inside for too long. I stuffed it in my waistband to go through it at my leisure later.

I took another look around, but nothing else caught my attention. I opened the entry door slowly and looked in the hall. Still no one around. I locked the door and went out to my car, the second packet of paperwork under my arm.

ELEVEN

There was still no else around, but even so, I walked quickly to my car, not taking the chance of someone looking out a window and calling the police. Once inside, I pulled the papers from my waistband and combined them with the other packet, placing the whole thing under the passenger seat.

As I left the back lot and came around the side of the building that led out, I noticed a squad car sitting in the lot across the street. I pulled out of the driveway and turned left, heading toward the main drag that would take me to the Merritt. Glancing in the rearview mirror, I watched as the cruiser pulled out and started following me. He stayed back about 30 yards and was there until I got to the entrance for the parkway. As I turned to go up the ramp, he continued straight, but the wave of paranoia that had come over me was strong. It might have been a coincidence, but it didn't feel that way. More like a silent warning. I racked my brain on the drive back to New Haven, trying to figure how they seemed to know exactly where I would be. I didn't want to believe they tagged my car, but I couldn't figure out any other method that would let them know where I was. I pulled into the rest stop in North Haven and parked far from the building, getting out to look under the car and inspecting the wheel wells. There was nothing I could spot. I got back in the car and sat for a few minutes until the feeling passed, then got back on the highway, taking it all the way through the tunnel and getting off at the New Haven exit.

By the time I got to the parking garage next to my apartment, I was royally pissed off. I couldn't shake the feeling that there was a lot more to this than I was seeing and that a much larger number of people were involved, including the cops. I found a space on the third level, parked, grabbed the paperwork from under the seat, and went down the stairway that led to College Street, coming out mid-block.

Before I got to the main entrance to my building, I looked over at the Owl and could see people sitting in the newly expanded outdoor area. Small miracles. I decided I would change my clothes, shower, and go see if I could maybe snag a seat. I needed a drink, badly.

Once inside, I checked my messages, but no one had called. I took a bottle of water out of the fridge and downed it all at once, getting a slight brain freeze. I kept my fridge colder than normal. The fleeting pain I experienced was a small price to pay for how the ice-cold water quenched my thirst.

I showered, got dressed in a pair of light sweat pants and a t-shirt, and then went to the Owl, bringing the paperwork with me. The crowd had thinned a little, and there was a small table for two open, so I went to sit down. It was a nice summer evening with only a moderate breeze, so I felt comfortable that I could look at the paperwork in relative peace. A waitress I didn't recognize came out after I was sitting there for a minute. The owner had begun making the employees wear vests with name pins. Her tag informed me her name was Amanda.

"Hey there. These tables are really for two people, but I don't think it'll get too busy for another hour or so, so you can sit here now, but if it does get busy, I may have to ask you to leave. Is that okay?"

It made me laugh. Rules.

"I guess it'll have to be. Thanks."

The sarcasm was lost on her and she smiled and nodded.

"Good. What'll you have?"

I ordered a Corona with a lemon instead of lime. I would hold off on the harder stuff until later in the evening. She nodded again and went inside.

I opened up the packet and spread the papers out in front of me. Like I'd noticed when I looked at them quickly in the apartment, most were insurance policies, car and life and health. The life insurance surprised me. It was for a hundred thousand dollars on Earl, and the beneficiary was Shana, with a rider that the monies go to Carla to hold in trust as her guardian until Shana turned 18. There was a clause that allowed some of the money to be used for her upbringing. If Earl turned up dead and hadn't just taken off, that money would be paid to Carla and Paul.

Amanda came back with my Corona, but there was a lime stuck in the neck. I pulled it out and asked her if she could bring me a lemon like I'd asked for. I heard a tongue click but she turned and went back inside, coming out a minute later with three small slices of lemon on a paper dish. I thanked her and got back a terse "no problem." She turned away and started sanitizing the table next to me where a couple had just departed. The aroma from the disinfectant was strong, and I winced and coughed. The two couples sitting on the patio both looked over at me, shooting me hard stares. I put up my hands in surrender, pushed a piece of lemon into the bottle, and took a long pull. It was cold and tasted good, social distancing aside.

Putting the paperwork into piles enabled me to go through each piece thoroughly and take notes if any questions came up. I would definitely ask Carla about the life policy. I put the other policies in that pile and looked through the rest. There were some love letters Earl had written to Janet. There was an envelope containing copies of all their birth certificates as well as their Social Security cards. A few property taxes bills on their cars, all marked paid. The registration for the Malibu.

The next piece of paper I found was interesting. In a small cardboard sleeve, there was a contract for a Lo-Jack device. Developed as the antithesis of "hijack," it was a system that was popular in the 80s and 90s, when an unusual number of cars were being stolen. The system involved installing a small radio device on a car that could then be tracked by a paired device that police cars were outfitted with. It worked well for a while, but recently as the costs went up, the company began selling it to insurance companies to monitor driving habits. The ACLU got involved, and the company went silent in the last few years. If Earl's car still had the device installed, it might be located using the tracker.

The only dilemma was finding a police department whose cars still had the trackers installed and were willing to help. I was pretty sure the Wallingford police department was out.

I looked up when I heard someone clearing her throat. It was Amanda.

"Another Corona?"

I looked at the bottle and was surprised it was empty. Sleep drinking.

"Sure, and please make sure..."

She finished for me. "I know, lemon, not lime." I got a big smile as a kicker. Winning hearts and minds.

I made a separate pile for the Lo-Jack contract and continued going through the papers until I found one toward the bottom that surprised me. Folded into thirds and tucked inside a blank envelope was a diploma, dated June 2017, congratulating Earl on his graduation from the Connecticut State Police Academy.

It also confused me. Carla told me he had flunked out. He was driving for Veyo, making a few hundred bucks a week. If he graduated from the academy, why wasn't he working as a state cop? Did he change his mind, thinking it was too difficult or too dangerous? Did he start the job and then get fired? Janet was still alive then...did she make him quit?

My reverie was interrupted by Amanda, bring back my beer with a lime in the neck, along with my tab.

"We're gonna need the table, the manager asked me to move you along."

I looked over her shoulder and saw the new manager watching us. I smiled and put down a 20, telling her to keep the change. I gathered the paperwork and stretched the elastic band back around the stack.

Removing the lime from the neck, I picked a lemon off the plate she'd brought before and put it in my mouth, downed the beer in one long gulp, sighing loudly afterwards for the benefit of the other patrons. I took the lemon out of my mouth and put it back on the plate, saluted the manager in the window, then walked back across the street to my apartment, thinking about going to Trinity Bar the entire time.

TWELVE

When I got inside, I could see that the light on my message machine was blinking. I picked up the message and heard Carla speaking very slowly, as if she was having trouble catching her breath.

"Tommy...Mr. Shore...it's Carla Vitter. I've been...talking to my husband...and he...we've decided that we no longer...need your services. I do appreciate everything that you've done...for us and, of course...please keep the money I gave you...for your trouble. I'm sorry. "

The phone disconnected quickly, like someone was standing next to her with a finger on the phone plunger, pressing it before she could say anything else. I called her back but got a busy signal.

I was at odds with what I should do. I really didn't feel like driving all the way back out there, but I was also concerned that Carla was in trouble. And I couldn't call the cops.

I tried the number again. This time I got a dial tone

and after a few rings, she picked up. I heard a weak "Hello" and a cough.

"Carla, it's Tommy. Are you okay? I just got your message. You didn't sound good."

I heard a deep sigh. "Mr. Shore, things have gotten complicated. Paul is upset that I hired you. He asked me to tell you that we no longer need your services. He's adamant about it."

Adamant. Code for abusive and threatening? I needed to tread lightly.

"Carla, I understand completely. In my business, I often run into people who take issue with strangers poking around in their business. Paul seems like that type. The thing is, I think there's more here than meets the eye. My feeling is that Earl was into something dangerous, for reasons outside of what it might seem like on the surface. I'd really like to continue looking into it."

There was a long pause. Finally, she said, "You said 'was.' Do you think Earl is dead?"

I took my time considering what to say to her.

"I think there's a good chance that he is. However, without a body, without a vehicle, without any kind of real evidence, it will be tough to prove that. That said, I have a few leads that might help me get some answers, so I'm going to continue looking. You don't have to pay me, and you don't have to mention it to Paul. However, I'd like to ask you a personal question. You can say it's none of my business, but I feel that we have something of a relationship now. I need to know, do you feel safe, for yourself and for Shana?"

I could hear her catch her breath. I didn't really want to have this conversation over the phone, but I had a sense that it would go badly in person, especially if her husband was around. She finally answered.

"Mr. Shore, Paul has his faults, he's not perfect. He used to drink a lot in the past, but he's given that up. I know he fights with his demons daily, but he's been sober for over five years now. I've asked him to start attending those meetings again, but he won't do it, says he doesn't like the crowd there, says they're all a bunch of crybabies."

She fell short of saying that he didn't hurt her or that she felt safe. I decided to change the subject back to what I had originally been hired to do, try to make her see the need.

"Look, I want to follow these leads down, see what happens. Once I do that, I will find a way to get the information to you. You can decide how you want to proceed. How's that sound?"

I knew she was the type who had a hard time saying no, and I felt bad for taking advantage of that. But someone needed to act here, and I figured it was me.

"Okay." She said it so softly I barely heard it, so I asked her to repeat it.

"Okay. But please don't come to the house again. Between you and that detective, it's made Paul so nervous and angry, I don't know what he'll do if he sees you at the house again."

She had slipped in that someone had come to investigate. "A detective came to the house, looking into Earl's disappearance?"

"Yes. Older man named Decker. He asked the same questions you did, and Paul got even more upset. That's why he told me to fire you. Decker said he would look into it but not to get our hopes up. Paul asked him how long before he would be declared dead. When Decker said it could be a year or so, Paul went crazy and asked him to leave."

Of course. Without a death notice, it would be hard to cash in the insurance policy. I had assumed they knew they were beneficiaries, but I was reconsidering whether Carla knew that. And it seemed like Paul was already sure that Earl was dead. I felt a wave of exhaustion come over me and wanted to end the call, now that I knew she was okay.

"Carla, if you need to talk to me about anything, please, don't hesitate to call me. Day or night. My cell is always on. Like I said, as soon as I know something after looking into these leads, I'll find a way to contact you. Sound good?"

She agreed and we hung up.

I considered going down to Trinity for a nightcap, but my heart wasn't in it after the call. I took out a package of shaved beef from the freezer and threw it in the microwave. When it was soft, I took down my All-Clad frying pan, tossed some butter in it, put it on the stove on a medium heat, and added the meat to cook. I lathered up half a loaf of French bread I had picked up earlier with mayo and put it aside. When the meat was ready, I placed three slices of Provolone on the top and covered the pan for a few seconds until it melted, then put the whole thing on the bread and brought it to the table. I opened another Corona, wishing I had the fore-thought to bring the lemon slices off the plate at the Owl. I sat and ate and thought about next steps, but my mind was racing.

When I was done and everything was cleaned up, I sat in the easy chair to try and watch something on

Netflix, but nothing held my attention. I was anxious about what I had found and eager to follow the leads. Hopefully without getting hurt.

Which reminded me that I needed to get some protection. Something small but effective. The hardware I had previously used had been confiscated by the police on my last case, and I never got around to replacing it. Going through usual channels would take too much time that I didn't have so, I decided to call my friend Mickey.

I met Mickey when a judge ordered both of us to complete our community service by talking to high school kids about how to control their tempers. We had both been before the judge for not being able to control ours. They assigned us to Wilbur Cross High School and, after each of us gave our talk, we went out for coffee. We liked each other for various reasons and stayed friends ever since, if you could call it that. He always told me to call him for whatever I needed, no matter the legality. I was discerning about how often I took advantage of that, but he had come through for me every time. For a price, of course.

The word on the street was he had his hand in almost everything nefarious. There was talk he was connected, which I definitely believed. There were other rumors that he was a CIA/FBI/DEA agent, which I didn't believe.

Mickey picked up on the first ring, and after I identified myself, we went through the usual rigmarole of hanging up and him calling me back on a burner phone. He wasn't so much paranoid as meticulously careful. It had worked for him for years. He hadn't done jail time for a long while. When he called me back, it was like a few days had passed instead of months.

"Tommy boy! Been too long. Missed seeing that mug of yours. Crazy thing, this bug. What's shaking and whattya need?"

Straight and to the point.

"Hey, Mick. Not much shakin', just getting back into it after the long vacation. You?"

He laughed. "No vacation for the wicked. I've been busy the entire time. No rest for the weary. Whattya need?"

I filled him in on the particulars of the new case. He listened without saying a word. It was one of things I liked about him. When you talked to him, you had his complete attention. I told him I need some personal protection, something that could be easily hidden, along the lines of my leather sap and maybe a small handgun. He laughed.

"Old-school, right? Well if I remember correctly, you bought that sap you used overseas, Ireland or some-place like that? Laws aren't as strict there. It's a hard get in the States. A lot of jurisdictions consider it deadly force that can cause serious head damage, and you're in the wrong state. Connecticut says it's illegal...now, if you were in Alabama or Maine? No problem."

Now it was my turn to laugh, mostly about how he knew this stuff. He continued.

"How about a set of brass knuckles? Law's kinda vague on those, and I've got plenty of 'em around here. Of course, I can always get you a piece."

I thought about it for a minute. Having some protection like that would be smart. I would need to be careful while dealing with the cops, but I would definitely want something that gave me an advantage if I ended up dealing with the fringe groups. Like a friend used to say, easier to ask forgiveness than permission. I told him I would take whatever he thought would work for me. He said okay, that he would work on the other thing and get back to me. Jokingly, I said, "If only you had access to a Lo-Jack scanner, I'd be all set."

He didn't laugh. Instead, he told me, "I actually do have access to one. Got an old cop car I bought at auction. Pretty sure there's one still in there."

It surprised me.

"Mick, any chance I can use that car? I would only need it for a few hours, just to drive around an area to try and locate a vehicle."

He paused. "Tom, I can't let you drive it, it's not registered but how about I send one of my guys to pick you up and take you where you need to go? That way, if you get stopped, it's on me and not you. I would feel better about it."

"That'll work. But it needs to be soon. Feels like this whole thing could go cold any minute now, so I would want to start fast. I have a location we can start at."

He didn't hesitate. "Sure. I'll send my guy to pick you up first thing in the morning, maybe 9:30? He'll have the other stuff with him, too."

This was a real break, and I was grateful. "Thanks, Mick. Let me know what I owe ya?"

"The hardware will be a couple of Benjamins. The car is on me. I hate it when kids are involved, especially little ones, so I'm happy to help. Talk soon."

We hung up and I sat back, surprised once again. Everybody has a soft spot, even Mickey.

THIRTEEN

The next morning, Mick's guy was waiting for me when I came out from the main entrance to my building, idling in a space right in front. The car Mickey sent was a 2008 Ford Crown Victoria that had been scrubbed of all the insignias on both the sides and the trunk. It had once been a dark blue but both the hood and roof had faded badly, so it looked like it was two-tone. It had a dealer plate stuck in the back window.

The driver didn't look to be much more than 25. He had longish hair and was wearing black Ray Ban wraparounds with mirrored lenses. Playing into the whole cop vibe.

I got in on the passenger side. He introduced himself as Jimmy. I almost put out my hand to shake his but forgot we no longer did that now. He caught the movement and laughed.

"Nice to meet you, Tommy. Where to?"

It was snug in the front seat. The car had a completely intact Interceptor console from its days as a police cruiser. The tracking computer was positioned in the middle, switched on and ready to be used. I had the coordinates from the Lo-Jack contract I'd taken from Earl's lock box.

I guided him through town to the Merritt Parkway. Neither of us spoke for a good fifteen minutes until I piped up.

"Do you know how to work the tracking computer?"

He nodded. Jimmy didn't say much. True to being one of Mickey's guys.

How about I buy us breakfast?"

He kept his eyes straight ahead on the road. Or at least I thought he did.

I stared at him and didn't say anything until he turned slightly to look toward me and asked, "I don't eat breakfast, but I can certainly take you wherever you want to go."

"What? I'm shocked. Most important meal of the day. What are you, 30?" I turned away, feigning disgust.

He laughed. "I'm 32. And some nutritionists say that's a myth, that intermittent fasting is actually a better way to go."

I turned back toward him and looked closer. I could see now he was a body builder or an MMA fighter, or some such thing. I asked him if he trained.

"I do. I'm a boxer. Middleweight. I work out at the boxing gym Mickey owns."

I wasn't aware Mickey had a gym, but it didn't really surprise me. I was sure he had his hand in a lot of enterprises. I refrained from making a "Rocky" joke about Mick's gym.

I had him get off at the same exit for Carla's place but turn left at the light instead. The road we were on forked around, and we followed it for a few miles until we came to Neil's Donuts. It was one of my favorite road places. They made killer bacon, egg, and cheese sandwiches and served them on bulkie rolls they baked in the back. It was a substantial breakfast, and the coffee they sold was pretty good, too.

Jimmy pulled in to the lot and had to jockey around a bit to find a space. I offered again.

"Can't get you anything?"

He paused, looked at me, and said he'd take a coffee, a mercy order. I sighed and went in to the shop, coming out 10 minutes later with two coffees, my BEC, and some donuts for later. One never knows.

I ate my sandwich, and we both drank our coffee. When we were done, I pulled out the Lo-Jack contract. Jimmy took it from me and punched in the coordinates. The computer whirred and then began emitting a soft beeping sound. I put the address I'd gotten from Nick at Veyo, the last place Earl logged in from, into the Waze app on my phone.

The Waze app took us down to Route 5, the main drag, near a Super Walmart. About a half mile past that, we turned left and followed that for about a half mile, crossing over the railroad tracks and coming into another industrial area. We drove until the road ended, then turned left again onto a road that took us into a wooded area. There was a street sign marked Parker Road, but half of it was covered by weeds and grass.

You had to look close to even notice it. There had only been a few houses at the beginning of the road, and they got fewer and farther apart as we followed the road. The road narrowed even more another half mile down and then stopped at a small cul-de-sac. There were a few old houses scattered around, but they looked abandoned and had seen better days. Behind the houses were woods.

The beeping sound got louder as soon as we turned down the road and remained steady. I asked Jimmy to pull over so I could get a better look around. Getting out of the car, I could see that one of the dilapidated shacks was practically in the woods. As I moved closer, I could also see that there was a pathway to the shack. Tall grass that had grown high around had begun to bend, covering the walkway. You had to push your way through to move it. Having never been a big fan of nature, I was hesitant to go up there. Connecticut was ripe with copperhead snakes that love this kind of environment. Or so I'd read.

Jimmy opened his door and was standing behind it, watching me decide what to do. I moved closer to the car, stopping near the front. He pointed his chin toward the shack. I could tell he wasn't a big fan of nature, either.

"Whaddya think? Worth going up there to take a look around? Signal's still strong here."

"Yeah, I'm going up to take a closer look. Stay here and watch the road? I'm not sure where this will lead, and I doubt there'll be trouble, but I would feel better knowing that you were keeping an eye on things out here. Good?"

He reached inside the car, opened the compartment between the seats, and pulled out a small revolver. After checking that it was loaded, he reached across the hood and handed it to me.

"As requested."

I took it and nodded again, then tucked it in the back of my waistband and headed toward the shack.

As I got within 50 feet, I could see that the path veered off to the right of the shack and the tall grass ended at twenty feet, changing to dirt. It looked more like a driveway, and after that the path turned into a makeshift road. Trees had been cleared, and it seemed possible you could get a car through there to the back of the shack and beyond. I could see that a car had definitely been driven up this way, straddling the path on both sides, headed toward the shack but seemed to only be going one way. It didn't look as though a car ever came back out, at least not this way, and someone had intentionally pushed the grasses over the tracks to cover them up.

I inhaled deeply and decided to go up to where the woods began. Walking slowly and cautiously, I listened intently for any sounds that meant danger, hissing, or rattling. By the time I got to the dirt tract surrounding the shack, I was sweating profusely. I looked back at Jimmy, who just saluted at me.

I decided to check out the shack first. I moved toward the first window and tried to look inside. The window was covered with dirt and grime as well as old pieces of plastic that had been nailed up hastily to cover the parts of the panes that were broken. I couldn't really see anything inside, so I sidled to the second window. It was farther away from the path. All of the panes were intact. The window wasn't much cleaner, but I could see inside a little better.

It looked to be a workshop. I could see a bench with an ancient vise grip attached to it and an old, rusty bow saw hanging on a nail behind it. Other than that, there wasn't much else, except garbage all over the floor, old newspapers, and a large number of dirty oilcloth remnants. My first thought was that no one had been in there in a while.

I went around to the back, and it was more of the same, except there was a door in the middle of the shack. It was the only way in or out. The door had a rusty chain on it with an even rustier lock that was holding the chain together. It was useless security. The thin panels at the bottom of the door had been kicked in, leaving two small openings. The shack was most probably used by little kids who could climb through those openings, a hide-out or a place to sneak smokes. An adult would have a hard time crawling through.

I knelt down and tried to get a better look inside. The other end of the place that I couldn't see from the first window was now more visible, and I could see another bench against the wall. It was lower, as if for seating. As my eyes adjusted, I could make out something above the bench, and my heart raced when I realized they were chains. Almost at the same time, I caught a whiff of an odor that I knew only too well. Copper. Blood. This place had been used for some kind of killing.

My knees started to hurt from crouching so I stood up and paused to think. Maybe I was being paranoid. The shack could have been used for hunting, for butchering deer or whatever else they caught around here, but it didn't feel like that. In the words of Joe Heller, just because you're paranoid doesn't mean they aren't after you.

I started to go back to the car when I glanced to the left and saw tire tracks in the wet ground leading away from the house and heading down toward another clearing. It had also been hastily covered up with brush. I walked the twenty yards down to it and pulled away enough brush that would let me fit through. Another twenty yards down from there was a chain across the road that had been lowered to let a car through and never raised back up. The Keep Out sign that had hung in the middle of the chain was lying in mud. I stepped over it and moved down toward the end of the road.

It started getting buggy, and I could smell the putrid odor of brackish swamp water. Another 20 yards down and the road came to an abrupt end at a small pond. The pond was maybe 50 feet in diameter, and the water had turned an ugly green-gray. The smell got stronger as I drew closer, and I knew I couldn't stay there long. I scanned the shoreline, trying to see if there was anything around of interest, but nothing caught my attention.

None of my questions had been answered, and I was ready to leave. I couldn't explain the beeping noises that led us here but figured we could drive around a bit and see if there were any other places that might lead to something. The weather had changed to oppressively hot, typical for July. It felt like the temperature had risen 10 degrees since we'd first arrived. The sun was high overhead, and the evaporation off the pond was making the air brutally thick with moisture. I needed to get out of there, but as I turned to leave, my sunglasses caught a reflection coming off metal. I turned back around and could see the glint was coming from the pond. I moved as close to the edge as possible without getting wet, trying to see what it was. There, almost in the middle of the pond, just breaking the top of the water, was the tail end of a car. You could miss it if you just glanced at it, but as I focused, I could make out a bit of the back end and the insignia. It was a Chevy Malibu.

FOURTEEN

My mind raced with the possibility that it could be a coincidence that it could be someone else's car, but I knew in my heart it was Earl's. The only question was what to do next. There was no telling how long it had been in the water, but if Earl had been sent into the pond in the car, he was surely dead.

This was now a crime scene. I thought back to every movement I'd made since leaving Jimmy. I had been careful not to touch anything at the shack. There would be no fingerprints to worry about. The ground was damp, but I had stayed as much on the grass as possible so forensics wouldn't be able to identify footprints. Satisfied that it was safe, I moved quickly back to the car I came in.

Jimmy was sitting inside the car with the engine running, the air conditioning turned all the way up. I got in and told him quietly, "We need to get out of here. Drive slowly." He didn't question it, pulled a U-turn, and drove back the way we had come in.

When we got back to the main road, I asked him to

pull into the first parking lot he saw at one of the industrial buildings that we'd passed. He found a shaded area toward the back of a cleaning company, under a grove of trees. Putting it into park, he waited for me to tell him what was going on.

My throat was dry. There was coffee left in my cup from breakfast, so I pulled off the lid and downed it. It was tepid, but the liquid felt good and would help me relay the story. My mind was racing, trying to figure out the next moves. I turned to face him.

"Do you have a burner phone in the car?"

He reached into the back seat and grabbed a Verizon bag, brought it into the front, and took out one of two burner phones. Both were new and still in the original packaging. He tossed the bag with the remaining phone into the back seat then reached into his pocket and pulled out a card with prepaid minutes on it. He opened the package and turned the phone on. When it was up and ready, he looked at me.

"We've got fifteen minutes. Who do you want to call?"

I told him about everything I saw and smelled at the shack and about discovering the car in the pond, adding in that I made sure not to touch anything. He listened intently and nodded that he understood.

"Do you think that whoever sent the car into the water tortured your guy before killing him?"

It was asked matter-of-factly, with no emotion in his voice. A gentle reminder that this was the world these guys lived in every day.

I shook my head.

"I don't even know that he was in the car. None of this makes much sense. Why would they grab the guy? I can't imagine what kind of information he would have that someone else could possibly want enough to kill him. If someone brought him out here to dump the car... if he was into something that he got caught with...if they used the shack to get information out of him...I don't know. There's too many if's that don't add up."

I realized that I was venting out loud, but I couldn't stop. Seeing the car had shaken me up. To his credit, Jimmy listened and didn't say anything. I continued my diatribe.

"The cops need to be brought in on this, right? Although I'm pretty sure some of them are involved in whatever *this* is. Shit, they could be the ones who dumped the car there in the first place. I need to get this out there, get it around, so they can pull the car out and see if Earl's in there, right? It's a friggin' crime scene."

Jimmy cleared his throat, indicating he wanted to make a suggestion. I looked at him and waited. He spoke calmly.

"How about this? We make an anonymous call to the local paper, get some reporter to come out here looking around? Small town like this, I'm betting somebody there would jump at this story. When they find what you found, they'll call it in and the cops would need to get involved. Done deal."

I thought about it for a minute. It sounded like a good plan, but the only paper in the area I knew about was a small-time rag out of Meriden. Still, there could be someone there who was itching to do more than reporting on local fairs or traffic stops. I googled the *Record-Journal* and found the name of a staff reporter who occasionally did some of the more hard-hitting stories, Glenn Burnett. I called the number listed but

got a recording that told me everyone was out of the
building until further notice. The recording also told
me I could leave a message for all members of the staff
and ticked off the numbers associated with names.
When it got to Glenn, I hit the number and it started to
ring. I was thinking about what message to leave when
someone picked up.

"*Record-Journal,* this is Glenn. How can I help
you?"

Hearing a live voice threw me at first. I tried to
collect my thoughts quickly. I wanted to tell him about
the car in the water, hopefully get him to send someone
out there or at least alert the Wallingford cops. I tried to
sound both fearful and excited, taking on the persona of
someone who had stumbled onto a story.

"I need to report something. I was hiking and bird-
watching near Parker Road in Wallingford off the
industrial road and was near these woods there. I found
this abandoned shack. When I looked inside, there was
nothing in it, but it smelled really bad. Then I noticed a
pond that was behind it. I went to get a closer look and
could see there was a car in the water. You gotta call the
cops or come down and see it for yourself. There could
be somebody inside it!"

"Okay, calm down. Where was this?"

"Parker Road in Wallingford. Where the road ends.
Hurry!"

I hung up in the middle of his asking my name.
Hopefully, he didn't think it was a crank call then send
someone else. I really wanted him to call the cops.

I handed the phone to Jimmy, who took it, broke it
apart, then put the pieces in the side pocket of his door.
I looked at him, confused.

"We'll toss it later, in different places."

I nodded and said, "Do you think he'll send somebody?"

Jimmy shrugged. "My guess is he'll call the cops to take a look and then come down himself if they find something. Even in a one-horse town like this, the possibility of a story outside of the usual boring shit has gotta be worth investigating. We can wait here and see if anybody comes."

I nodded again, impressed. He swung the car out from beneath the shade and over to where a few more cars were parked in the lot, facing the street. There was only one way to Parker Road, and if the cops came to investigate, we would see them.

They came quickly. Not twenty minutes had passed when a squad car sped by us and turned down toward Parker. We continued to wait. I wanted another coffee or, better yet, a drink. Another fifteen minutes went by, and another squad car came past, also speeding down toward Parker. The reporter must have believed me and done exactly as we hoped, calling it in, but I was surprised at how fast they turned up. Ten minutes later, a tow truck showed up, followed by an unmarked. The driver of the unmarked looked like Decker, with someone else in the passenger seat. Probably the other detective. I lowered myself down into my seat as they went by.

I told Jimmy to leave. They would pull the car out of the pond and spend a fair amount of time looking at the scene. It could be hours before they brought the car anywhere. Part of me wanted to wait and see if they called for an ambulance or the coroner's vehicle but I knew we were too conspicuous sitting where we were.

Jimmy pulled out of the lot and headed back toward Route 5. I saw a blue Toyota Camry speed past us, heading toward the scene, and watched in the side view mirror as it turned down toward Parker. I was betting it was the reporter.

It was mid-afternoon and the sun was brutal. I needed to calm down. I asked Jimmy if he was hungry or thirsty and offered to buy him lunch. He shrugged and said, "I could eat." I had read about a BBQ joint in town that made Kansas City-style ribs and lots of other stuff. I found the Pig Rig online and followed the directions down the main drag.

We almost missed the turnoff and might have ended up going north to Hartford, but Jimmy saw the road sign and was able to veer in at the last minute. We drove another 50 yards and turned into a strip mall. Toward the back, I could see a food truck and behind it, the restaurant.

It was owned by a guy who had served in the army scouts and catered to vets. We went in, ordered a platter of various meats and sides, and took a seat in the restaurant, away from the counter. The walls were decorated with rock-and-roll memorabilia, leaning toward the classic hard-rock genre. We found a booth next to a wall with two Journey t-shirts tacked to it.

The food came and it was perfect. Moist brisket, delicious ribs, creamy mac-n-cheese, and coleslaw with a vinegary bite, all washed down with black cherry Polar Seltzer. We ate in silence for a while.

When Jimmy was done, he sat back in the booth and looked at me still eating.

"Man, you really like to eat, don't ya?"

I was gnawing on a rib bone and didn't look up,

nodding instead and said, "Yep, I eat every day. Helps me think."

He laughed and waited until I was done. When I finally pushed my plate away, he asked, "So, what's next?"

I looked at him and downed the rest of the seltzer, not answering his question. I had noticed a couple of uniforms come in to get lunch and didn't want to take any chances.

"Not here. Let's go. Take me back to my apartment."

We walked out quickly. The cops looked at us as we left. They didn't come out as we got in the car, but my heart was racing and my paranoia was turned up to 11.

We got on the highway and were back at my apartment in twenty minutes, neither of us saying much. I thanked Jimmy for helping me out and asked him to let Mickey know that I would be calling him shortly.

He nodded and didn't say anything. I got out and he sped off down the street.

The apartment was hot from the afternoon sun, so I cranked up the air and stripped down to skivvies. I opened up my old laptop to get more information on Glenn Burnett and the kinds of stories he wrote. His byline came up quickly, and I saw immediately I'd gotten the right reporter. He had written a number of stories on murders and deaths and about corruption at town hall. I was surprised at the amount of crime there was to be written about, but the paper covered Meriden, Wallingford, and nine other neighboring towns. There was even some overlap with Hartford that touched on the politics of Meriden.

I closed the computer and looked at the clock on the

stove. Ten minutes to five. I got up and went into the bathroom to shower, to wash the day off my skin. I would check the paper online in the morning to see if anything had been written about the car, then try to reach out to Burnett. It was doubtful he would talk to me, but you never know. Right now, I needed a drink.

FIFTEEN

Sitting in Trinity's courtyard, I decided I would try to smoke a cigar, then changed my mind when I looked at the neighboring tables and saw people eating early dinners. I had walked the three long blocks from the apartment in the remaining heat of the late afternoon, and the refreshment of the shower had dissipated quickly. Trinity's inside bar was still open to limited seating but I saw a table just inside the patio gate near the street. I grabbed that, hoping there'd be a cooling breeze until the sun went down. I wasn't there five minutes when Megan came over.

"Hi, Tommy. Welcome back. Usual?"

Megan was a little shy and quiet, but she had a great smile and was a very good waitress, attentive but never hovering. I gave her a big smile and said yes, and she went to get me a Corona and a Jameson pour.

I watched people walking by until Megan brought my drinks, along with a menu.

"It's new, smaller, but we still have those wings you love. Should I put an order in?"

They made killer wings with honey and mustard and some kind of exotic pepper on them, but I was still full from lunch.

"No, I'm good for now. Maybe in a while."

I sipped the Irish whiskey first, then took a long hit of the beer. It was ice cold and would have been perfect if I could light up. Instead, I stared at my phone for a while. There were no calls. I was expecting to hear from Carla once they alerted her to finding Earl's car but considered that the cops might wait a bit to let her know, until they had as much of the story as possible. I wasn't sure what I would get from Burnett tomorrow, but I was hoping I would get enough to convince Carla to let me continue. My "dog with a bone" streak had been triggered.

I sat back and started thinking about what got me doing this in the first place. It seemed like this virus thing and the subsequent quarantine got everyone rethinking their lives, and I was no different.

I spent most of my working life in very different businesses. After a short stint in the music biz, I met a guy who got me hooked up to go on the road as a book rep for a major publisher. It was a good gig with a lot of travel. I ended up spending twenty years doing it, until that business imploded and I found myself out of a job, along with scores of others. Not knowing what else to do, and having never been much for physical grunt work, I thought back on my love of detective fiction and mysteries and was naïve enough to assume I could do that as easily as anything else. I looked into the legalities, but there didn't seem to be many. The state required that you take a test to get licensed, but they wanted a lot of money to do it. So I didn't, figuring I could keep my fees low enough that anyone who hired me wouldn't ask too many questions. If they were somehow dissatisfied, they would chalk it up to "you get what you pay for." There had been few problems. I took out an ad, spent some time using social media and shortly had my first case, a cheating husband deal. It didn't take me long to catch him checking into a motel with another woman, take some pictures, and collect my $500. Much of it was boring work, sitting in a car and waiting until the moment I needed to act, but I liked it. It appealed to my inner lazy, shiftless side.

I had been married then to Katarina, a Russian woman I met in London when I was there for a trade show. She had been working as one of those beautiful women who stood in front of a booth and touted a product, getting interested people to come in. I was interested--but not in the product.

She agreed to go out with me that night after the show, and we got very drunk. Or, at least I did. She could hold her liquor better than anyone I'd ever met, and one thing led to another. I woke up the next morning with a hangover and a note, thanking me for my invitation to come visit me and stay at my house in the States. I couldn't remember a thing, but when I went back to the show and looked for her on the floor, the vendor she worked for had closed up and no one was around. I put it out of my mind, thinking it was a just a one-night-stand kind of thing.

When I got back home, barely a week went by before my phone rang. It was Katarina, on her way to Connecticut on the commuter train from New York. I picked her up at the New Haven station and brought her home with me. She didn't leave for five years. I heard about making her "an honest woman" almost every day, and we eventually had a civil service marriage at the town hall in New Haven. I thought I had grown to love her, but in retrospect, I hated being by myself more. It was a marriage of convenience for both of us.

She liked nice things, expensive things, and when the money got tight, the marriage started to fall apart. I was in New Haven often. She and I spent our time there drinking and dining. Rina, as I called her, started to hate the Owl Bar because "smoke makes hair smell bad," and she didn't like the type of people who frequented the bar, especially those I was friendly with. I started coming down alone. We soon divorced, almost as quickly as we had married, and she got the house, the car, and a bunch of other things we had purchased together. To her credit, she never asked for alimony, and I was able to sublet an apartment from one of the guys I met at the bar. It was directly across from the Owl and within walking distance of most of the city. The front room was both a living room and an office, and it worked well for my new endeavor.

I didn't need to make a lot of money. I had a fair amount of savings she didn't touch, and I was able to cash in the various 401ks that I'd had with the different publishers I'd worked for. I wasn't going to get rich, but I would be able to dine out most of the time and drink whenever I wanted.

I met some cops who frequented the bar, and they in turn introduced me to various lawyers and accountants who could throw business my way as needed. Compared to the licensed guys, I was inexpensive. Once the word got out that I was also diligent, organized, and tenacious, a fair amount of referral work came my way.

I also met Reilly at the Owl. I hadn't yet moved downtown and was in the bar early on a Friday night, about 8:00, when Reilly sauntered in, already three sheets to the wind from the previous bar where he's spent the afternoon. He was tall and gangly and dressed like someone who was clearly a fan of the Ramones or the Sex Pistols. He sat down at the end seat of the bar and was being loud, but not in a mean or obnoxious way. I would later discover the guy didn't really have a mean bone in his body. No, he was more of a drunken Irishman type, friendly and boisterous and happy. It was amusing to some of us watching from our seats near the cigar cases as he went back and forth with Summer, the bartender and manager at the time. Evidently, it wasn't amusing to others. Summer could give as good as she got, and she clearly had a soft spot in her heart for Reilly. But a couple of morons sitting at the bar misread it, and words were exchanged. Reilly tried to gently back down from it, but you could tell these two were aching for a fight. I stood up from my seat, and when one of them started to get up off his stool to get in Reilly's face, I came over, grabbed the punk's shoulder, and pushed him back down, hard. I didn't say anything, but the guy looked at me, and there was the recognition in his eyes that this wasn't going to go well for him. I had boxed most of my life and may have already assumed a stance that would make the most of a left cross. He mumbled something, his friend threw a 20 on the bar, and they left. Summer laughed and said the next one was on her. Reilly asked me to sit with him at the bar and we became great friends.

Over the years, he had become more difficult. He was in poor health and spent countless hours going to doctors to figure out what was wrong with him. Not one was able to come up with a proper diagnosis, and it made him cranky. He worked a tough, physical job, inspecting houses down in the wealthier part of Connecticut. It was his own business and he had grown it considerably, but good help was hard to find and he ended up doing much of the physical stuff himself. It took a toll.

He was always ready to party, though, and loved to drink hard, eat well, and "go on an adventure!" I'd involved him in a few of my more recent cases, the ones that had gotten difficult, and he'd even sent a client or two my way. When the pandemic hit, he went underground, and I hadn't seen him since. I was on my own for this one. Besides, he hated "the country," and I'm sure he would think that Wallingford was as country as it gets.

"Another round, Tommy?"

Megan was standing in front of me. She had asked me once already, but I was deep inside my reverie. When I finally focused, I looked down and saw both glasses were empty.

"Nah, just another beer. Lot going on tomorrow. But I will take ten wings to go for later and a check."

She nodded and left, and I looked around the patio. There were still a number of empty tables, but I still didn't feel totally comfortable smoking a cigar yet. Soon.

Ten minutes later, Megan brought the wings and my beer and a check. I gave her a 20 and a couple of singles. These folks had gone a while without a paycheck, and every little bit helped.

I sat there alone, drinking quietly. I had a weird feeling that I couldn't put my finger on. I would start again tomorrow by visiting the reporter to see what I could find out, then go over to Carla's and try to talk to her. Hopefully, with good news.

SIXTEEN

I got up around eight the next morning, showered, made a pot of strong coffee, then got the car from the garage and headed back out to Wallingford. Mark's car got great mileage, but I was aware that I had driven it more in the past week than I had driven all year and would need to fill the tank soon. If I remembered how to do it.

The newsroom for the *Record-Journal* was located on Broad Street, a main road that ran from Wallingford to Meriden. I headed toward the Merritt Parkway and got on heading north. I got off the Merritt at exit 66, turned right at the light, then followed the road up past a number of liquor stores, a Home Depot that was directly opposite a Lowe's, a Chick-Fil-A, and some other fast food joints, as well as at least four car dealerships and five strip malls. The building housing the *Record-Journal* was set back off the road, behind a strip of stores, including a Starbucks, a Verizon, and an AT&T store. I marveled that all of these places had been closed for the last five months and were only now beginning to come back to life. None of them looked very busy.

I stopped at a convenience store that was in one of the strip malls and purchased that day's *Record-Journal*. Most of the top headlines were national, centered on the country's recovery and where the remaining pockets of coronavirus were. Toward the bottom was a one-column headline over an article about a car that had been pulled out of a pond, describing the make and model. There was a line about how the police were investigating, but there was no mention of a body.

I parked in a visitor space near the entrance and went inside. There was no reception desk, only a security guard sitting on a chair behind a large wooden desk. He had a mask on and at first glance looked to be sleeping. As I moved closer, he stood up, yawned, and asked me to sign a visitor book. Old school. I signed and pushed it across the desk to him.

"Who ya here to see?"

"Glenn Burnett."

"Second floor. Straight ahead. Can't miss him." He chuckled.

I took the elevator to the second floor. I wasn't sure what I to expect, but this wasn't it.

There was no experience in my past that included spending any time in a newspaper editorial room, but I had grown up watching movies like "All the President's Men." I knew those films involved big city newspapers but this was the exact opposite.

It was a very small space filled mostly with cubicles, with a handful of outer offices and meeting rooms scattered about. From the looks of things, the paper was still not yet up to full steam. There was one woman sitting in a cubicle and a guy and a woman in the offices. I asked a young woman making copies at a machine near the elevator doors if she could point me to Glenn Burnett. She stopped what she was doing and walked me over to his office.

Glenn was eating his lunch, and as he looked up from his one of his Big Macs, I could tell he wasn't very happy I was there. He was a large man, maybe 6'5" and probably close to 320 pounds. He stood up as I walked into his office, and I could see he carried a lot of his weight in his gut. His olive-green shirt was barely tucked in, and he had thrown his brown tie over his shoulder to keep it clean as he ate. It was a losing battle. He looked up with a scowl.

"Can I help you? I know we don't have an appointment." It was clear he didn't want any visitors just now.

"Name's Tommy Shore. You're right, we don't have an appointment, but I need to talk to you about the car the police found in the pond at the end of Parker Road yesterday. I'm a private investigator."

He sighed, sat back down, picked up his lunch in the wrapping he was using as a placemat, opened a drawer, and put it all in there, slamming the drawer with aggravation. He opened another drawer and pulled out a small yellow legal pad and a pen.

"Okay, tell me what ya know."

I smiled. "I'm not actually here with information for you, although I might be able to shed some light on certain aspects of this. I'm here to see what you might be able to tell me about it."

He put the pen down, and I could hear a soft, guttural sound coming from his throat.

"Shore is it? I trust you read today's paper? What

makes you think I have any more information than what's in the article? And even if I did, why would I tell you? You haven't even shown me any credentials. As far as I'm concerned, you're some schmuck off the street, chasin' a buck."

He raised his voice and was getting madder by the second. His face reddened.

"Hey, Glenn, take it easy. It's been a while since I did CPR. Listen, I'm not looking for a score. I was hired by the family of a guy who went missing a little over a week ago. I'm pretty sure the car they pulled out of the pond yesterday was his, but I need to confirm it. There was nothing in the article about a body being inside, so if it was his, he's still missing. I was hoping the cops might have given you a VIN number or the registration that might have been in the glove box, something that they might have identified the owner with? And, of course, if there's anything else you might have found out."

He seemed to have gotten himself back under control. He sat back and considered me and what I was asking for.

"Have you spoken to the cops? There's a detective working the case, a waste of a guy named Decker. I've never had much luck with him, but maybe he'll tell a perfect stranger everything there is to know about the incident. Just go in and charm him. You seem like a charming guy to me."

I smiled at the sarcasm. I decided to try to win hearts and minds by appealing to his "we're in this together" side.

"Look, I know it's a rough time for guys like us. The Internet's eating everybody's lunch. I used to be in the book biz, same deal. Now I'm doing this. It's not glamourous, but it pays the bills. The guy I'm looking for has a little girl. She's already lost her mother. All she wants is to see her daddy, but it feels to me like he may have gotten himself into some pretty nasty stuff. Like I said, the cops won't help, they've actually threatened me, so I need help. Anything you can tell me would be great. Okay?"

He looked at me as if waiting for me to keep talking, but now it was me waiting for him to speak. An old "closing the sale" technique. After 30 seconds, he sighed and tossed the pad and the pen over to my side of the desk.

"Write down the names and your number and any particulars you think are key. I'll see what I can find out."

I did as I was told, smiled, thanked him, got up, and started to leave. But he had last words for me.

"Shore? If I can tell you anything, it's this...be careful. Wallingford may be a small town, but the cops in small towns, cops that are under the radar, they can be the most dangerous cops of all."

It was a weird thing to say to me, but I nodded and turned for the elevators. I could hear the drawer of his desk being pulled open and the crinkling of fast food paper. Priorities.

I took a backroad toward New Haven, planning to stop at Neil's Donuts to pick up a dozen I could bring to the bar that night. Route 5 split off and took me down a road that ran parallel to it and led to an entrance of the Merritt a few miles down so I could get back on toward home.

Neil's wasn't crowded, so it took me no time to grab

what I needed along with a couple for myself and a cup of coffee for the ride home. When I came out of the shop, I went to the passenger side of the car to put the box on the seat and put the coffee on the roof. Closing the door, I reached for the coffee and spotted an unmarked sitting in the back of the lot, under some trees, idling and waiting. It was a newish Chevy Caprice and could have been anybody's except for the red and blue lights in the grill and the spotlight below the side view mirror. There looked to be only one guy sitting in the car, the driver. I got back in my car, secured the coffee in the cup holder, and pulled out slowly. I was 200 yards down the road when I looked in the rearview mirror and saw the unmarked pull out from Neil's.

I kept to the speed limit and got on the highway, going through North Haven and Hamden and heading towards the New Haven exit after the tunnel. I kept checking. He had gotten on the parkway as well but I seemed to have lost him at the Mobil Gas stop just before the North Haven exit. I gave myself a ration of grief for being paranoid again and calmed myself with a blackberry jelly donut and some hot coffee.

Getting off the Merritt, I took Whalley Avenue all the way up to Broadway and down to my apartment. I found a space on the street in front of my building, put a couple of hours on the meter, and took everything inside. I planned to use the car again later.

Sam was on duty in the lobby. I walked over, opened the box of donuts, and offered him one. He shook his head.

"Lotta cholesterol in those, Tommy. My doctor says I need to watch myself."

Sam was in his mid-80s.

I shrugged, said, "Suit yourself," and went to my apartment, shaking my head. Everyone wants to live forever.

Once inside, I put the box of donuts and the coffee on the counter and hit the button to pick up messages. Carla's voice came through.

"Mr. Shore, this is Carla Vitter. I'm sure you've heard by now that they found Earl's car. That same detective came by to let us know. He thinks Earl's left the state, that he got rid of the car in the pond himself. I'm so confused, I don't know what to do. Please call me?"

There were two more calls from her without messages.

I was about to call her back when there was knock on my door. I looked through the keyhole and saw a man about thirty years old, in a beige suit and dark tie, holding up a badge.

"Mr. Shore? John Moreland. I'm a detective with the state police. I'd like to ask you a few questions."

I opened the door. He kept his badge out until he was satisfied that I had looked at it enough to know it was real.

"Mr. Shore, I'm the lead officer of an investigation into the disappearance of Earl Scosa. May I come in?"

I stepped aside and swept my arm around to indicate it was okay to enter. The call to Carla could wait.

SEVENTEEN

Moreland came in, moving into the middle of the living room, looking around and scanning everything as he did. I got the sense that he was being more careful than nosy. He turned toward me. I had closed the door and was in the kitchen area, standing behind the island that separated the two rooms. I opened the box of donuts.

"Donut, detective?"

He laughed and waved it off. My first sense was he was the easy-going type, but I'd been wrong about these things many times before.

He was young, maybe early 30s, and well-dressed but not in a showy way. His sport coat looked off the rack but fit him well, his khakis were pressed, and his shirt and tie matched perfectly. He even had cop shoes on, black Florsheim Oxfords, polished to a high gloss. He looked to be in great shape, and his blond hair was neat and trimmed. He seemed polite but to the point.

"What can I help you with, detective?"

He smiled and asked, "Can we sit, Mr. Shore? And please call me John."

It was my turn to smile. "That's usually my line. Sure, but only if you call me Tommy."

I moved around the counter and came over and sat down in my easy chair, sweeping my hand out to signal him to sit on the sofa. I was aware that I had made that gesture twice in the last two minutes. A regular Vanna White. He sat down and folded his hands together, prayer-like, resting them on one knee.

"Tommy, I understand you've been hired by the family of Mr. Earl Scosa to help find out what might have happened to him?"

I nodded. "Well, not so much the family as by Carla Vitter, his sister-in-law. Earl's late wife was her sister. Carla's husband, Paul? Not a fan. But my agreement was with Carla."

"Would you be willing to tell me what you've found out so far?"

I hesitated. I didn't want to tip my hand before I found out what this was about.

"How about we trade off? I answered your questions, you answer mine. I'll go first. What's the Connecticut State Police doing involved with this? I'm actually surprised the state police has detectives."

He looked at me and then looked away. I thought he might be staring out the window, but you couldn't really see much out there, save an alleyway that led down to Temple Street. I waited. After a minute, he looked back at me.

"Not many people know everything the state police does. Most folks think it's all about stopping speeders on the highway. Which is true, we are key to traffic enforcement, but we also do crime scene analysis, missing persons, investigate fringe groups, and anything else needed to protect the citizens of Connecticut."

He smiled. "Sorry if that sounded a little rah-rah."

I waved it off.

"Always great to hear someone who's passionate talk about work. Go on."

He had kept smiling through all this, but he paused, stopped smiling, and looked at me.

"Okay, here goes. Earl Scosa was an undercover agent for us. He was a graduate of the academy and was selected right afterwards to be part of an elite team that looks into crimes in this state where undercover is necessary. Crimes involving drugs or violence or corruption. This case involves all three. Your turn."

I gave him everything I had so far, from getting the call to finding the car and going to the paper. When I was done, I looked at him for a response, but there was nothing on his face. I got the sense that he had already known most of what I told him and was weighing it against what he knew.

"Tommy, I'm going to let you in on the background of this case. We've asked around about you, and we get the sense that you're a stand-up guy. The information I give you is highly confidential. Will you be willing to hear what I have to say and not share it with anyone?"

I picked up on the "we" and fought the urge to say, "Who would I tell?" but nodded instead. Moreland sat back on the couch and pulled a small envelope out of one of the side pockets of his jacket. He opened it, took out a handful of photographs, and tossed them on the makeshift coffee table in front of me.

I picked up the packet. Most of the pictures were of

groups of men gathered in a room. There was a podium at the front with someone standing behind it. It could have been a sales conference anywhere in the world. As I moved through the packet, there were separate shots of the guy behind the podium, by himself or with one other guy. There was one of him alone, sitting on a chair, away from the group.

"Who are these guys?" I went to hand the photos back to him.

"Did you take a good look at the men in the crowd?"

I shook my head and then went through them again, looking more closely this time. I realized what he was asking me about when I looked at the third photograph down. One of the men was Ron Decker, the detective I had gone to see who had sent the uniform to harass me. I was confused.

"I repeat, who are these guys?" I handed him back the photos.

He took them, straightened them out, put them back in the envelope and then back into his coat. He leaned forward and lowered his voice. The look on his face was stone cold. I leaned in a little myself.

"That's a recent meeting of the Knights of the Message. They're a satellite group that's affiliated with the Ku Klux Klan, based out of North Carolina. The guy sitting on the side is an organizer with that group. They've been in this area for quite some time, but we've only received information recently that they are planning to step things up and wreak havoc on a number of government buildings in Hartford and New Haven. There have been reports they have been stockpiling explosives and guns."

I sat back, stunned. My mind raced with the questions I needed to ask, but I couldn't gather them in my mind coherently. This was so much bigger than what I thought I was getting myself into.

Moreland could see I was knocked over.

"Tommy, I know it's a lot for anyone to take in. I'm going to pile on a bit and tell you that those pictures were taken by Earl Scosa. He had been undercover for us for a while and was gathering evidence about the group so we could arrest them before they did real damage. We had built a solid case that needed some finishing touches. We believe Earl was found out, tortured, and killed before he could finish this."

I didn't know where to start, so I asked him the tritest of questions.

"How did you guys find out about me?"

He nodded. "We knew about you from when you first went to see Carla. We had her phone bugged for some time. We believe her husband Paul might somehow be involved, although we're not sure exactly how. We've also been following you since you went to Earl's apartment. We had a guy watching the place and when you went there, we took the opportunity to tag the car you were driving. That car was registered to someone else, but we surmised you must have borrowed it. We put a monitor on it so we would know where you were and where you went."

I could feel my face redden as the anger flowed through me.

"You bugged my car?"

He looked at me and didn't answer, then sat back on the couch.

"Actually, we had to remove another device that

was already there. That one tracks back to the Wallingford police department."

I was stunned again, although it explained how the cops always seemed to know where I was or was going. I looked at Moreland and smiled.

"You're the unmarked Chevy Caprice on the Merritt."

Moreland nodded. I was beginning to feel that I was way over my head but pushed forward.

"So, what can I do for the state police?"

"We'd like you to pick up where Earl left off. No one you've come into contact with has any idea which side you're on. As far as they know, you stumbled onto this while trying to find out what happened to Earl. It's not farfetched that you could hold the same beliefs that these people have and would want to join them, now that you know they exist. All you'd need is an in, someone to vouch for you. Paul Vitter could be that person."

I jerked my head back when he mentioned the name. There was no way I could use Paul to infiltrate this group.

"John, Paul Vitter is a mean, vitriolic asshole who beats his wife. There's no way I could get close enough to him to make him feel comfortable enough to introduce me or vouch for me. I'd hurt him first. Sorry, that's off the table. I don't even trust him being around Earl's little girl."

He stared at me. "Do you have any proof of domestic abuse?"

I snickered. "Well, I don't have video of him hitting her but I've seen her face afterwards. I've seen abuse before, and all the signs are there. Plus, he's a moron that I'm betting is only allowing me to look into Earl's disappearance because he knows there's an insurance policy that has the little girl as the beneficiary and Carla as the guardian until Shana turns 18. It allows for monies from the payout to be used for her upbringing. I'm betting Paul will get hold of that cash long before Shana turns 18."

Moreland was looking down, shaking his head. When he looked up, it was back to business.

"So, can I convince you to do this, infiltrate this fringe group and help us put these guys in prison before a lot of people get hurt?"

I felt boxed in. There wasn't a way to say no outright that I could live with, but I needed to find another way to do this, a way that I could feel more comfortable with. It probably wouldn't make them happy, but it was my life on the line here.

"John, I need a day to think about it. Can I have that, can I get a day?"

I watched his face as he considered it. I couldn't read him.

Finally, he stood up, said "Sure. I'll call you tomorrow," then walked toward the door. I got up to let him out and held the door. He stopped halfway out and turned toward me.

"This is the part in the movie where my character says, 'We can't do it without you. Your country needs you.' Always sounded a bit trite to me. It is true, though. Earl's disappearance has set us back considerably, and we think something's going to happen soon, so I'm asking that you give this your utmost consideration."

I nodded. Utmost.

He walked down the hall and out into the lobby. I

locked the door, went to the cupboard, pulled down the bottle of Jameson, and then changed my mind. I needed to walk and get some air and think.

If I worked it right, I would end up at Trinity in time for an early dinner.

EIGHTEEN

It was a beautiful late afternoon when I left the apartment. The heat had broken early in the day, and there was a lovely breeze that cooled things off. I walked to Chapel Street and crossed kitty-corner to the New Haven Green. There were people out, many more than I'd seen on the streets in recent weeks.

A group of eight or so musicians formed a drum circle, all with various types of congas and bongos and even a steel drum. They were being careful to keep the proper distance but were working up a sweat, pounding out a hypnotic rhythm. A few people around the circle were dancing and letting themselves go. It felt good to see life back in the city.

I stopped and listened for a few minutes. It made me happy. Some people were still wearing masks, nervous about another wave coming but needing to be out in the world, experiencing other humans.

I walked across the green to Temple Street, passing first behind the United Church, then down the side walkway of Center Church, built in the early

1800s. I felt the history of it every time I was near it. Continuing on across the walkway in the middle of the block, I walked around the green area that usually hosted the New Haven Jazz Festival and the Arts and Ideas Festival. A few vendors had set up carts, and I stopped at one to get some gelato. It was a perfect accompaniment to the kind of day it was. The offerings were lemon, lime, or coconut, and I asked for a mix of all three.

I walked for a while down Church Street to Elm, then down Elm Street to State. It was quiet, and there were relatively few people on the streets. I headed up State Street until I got to the Elm City Market, then up Chapel and through the shortcut to Trinity. There was only one person sitting on the outside patio, close to the entryway. I took the same far-end table nearest to Orange Street.

I was struggling with what I should do, thinking back to what Moreland had said and asked. On the one hand, I felt an obligation, purely self-imposed, to Carla and, by extension, to Shana. Losing one parent was bad enough. Losing two changed you.

Both of my parents had died in a car accident when I was nine years old. They were coming back from visiting my father's father, who was in an assisted living home in Danbury. My father worked long hours to earn a living and was always tired. This particular Sunday, he was coming off a week where he had logged over 70 hours, but they never missed going up to see my grandfather. This week was no different. They typically used route 34, a winding, two-lane road that's used as a shortcut by large trucks going between New Haven and I-84. My father fell asleep at the wheel on the way back and hit a delivery truck head on. Both my parents were killed instantly.

They always left me with my aunt. She was a little high-strung, but she loved me and took good care of me. My mother's older sister, she had been living alone for as long as I could remember. I didn't know what divorce meant then, but she had a large yard I could play in and she'd play with me all day, so it was great. She'd make tomato soup from scratch with grilled cheese sandwiches each time I came, and we'd sit in front of the television together, watching *Davey and Goliath* or *Kukla, Fran, and Ollie* and eat our lunch. Later at night, after a dinner of either meatloaf or hot dogs, there'd be *Walt Disney's Wonderful World of Color*. My parents would arrive just as the show was ending, and the three would sit and have coffee and talk until it was over. I would come sit at the table and have "coffee milk," where my dad would put a few teaspoons of coffee in my milk glass so I could taste it. It started me on my love for coffee.

The Sunday they didn't come home, my aunt made up the spare room, and I went to sleep there. Long before cell phones, I was awakened by the phone ringing. It was late, but my Aunt has been up waiting, and I could hear her scream and start crying. I went downstairs to see what happened, and she hugged me for a long time before taking me back upstairs and telling me to go back to sleep. I didn't ask her about my parents, but I knew that something was wrong.

My aunt was never the same. When I came down the next morning, there were people in the house I didn't recognize, and she was still in her room, in bed. A man came out of her room carrying a black bag, and I was told by one of the next-door neighbors that I needed to be very quiet. When I asked her when my mom and dad would get there, she started crying.

It was a whirlwind after that. The man with the black bag came back later that afternoon and stayed in my aunt's bedroom for a long time. When he emerged, he looked at the neighbors and shook his head. There was a lot of whispering, and now the husband from next door took me for a walk up the block, telling me what had happened. I was confused and sad and angry and didn't really understand it all, but he made me promise that I would "behave and only whisper in the house."

When we went back inside, more people I didn't know had arrived, and I was aware that they were all staring at me. I went up to the spare room and got into bed. I couldn't stop shaking.

A few weeks later, different people came to get me. My aunt had had a nervous breakdown and couldn't take care of me anymore. I went into her bedroom to say goodbye, but she was sedated and burrowed deep under the covers, with one arm out and draped across the quilt. It was the last time I ever saw her.

After a short stay with the two strangers who took me to their house, I was put into the foster care system. In those days, older kids were hard to place, and I was almost 10 before my first placement.

The people who took me in the first time were older and already had two other foster kids and one of their own. There was trouble from the start, and I was soon returned, like an empty soda bottle. I was sent to two other homes, but it was more of the same, and I was now classified as "troubled."

I was 12 when I was sent to the last home. There

were two kids there, one each from the previous marriages of the mother and father. She was nice, but I could tell early on that her husband had a drinking problem. He would work until 5 then go to a bar with his cronies until 7:30 or 8. When he got home, he would get a "report" from the mom. If there had been any trouble from a child that kid would be sent upstairs to wait. He'd let fifteen minutes go by, then make a show of removing his belt so we could both see, then march upstairs. In a few minutes, we could hear the beating and the screaming. It would go on for a while. Afterwards, he would come downstairs, go to his makeshift bar by the television, pour a drink, and look at us, saying the same thing every time: "Let that be a lesson to you to be good or else."

I hated him.

It didn't happen to me as much as to the other two kids. There were regular check-ins from the DCS, who would ask questions and check for irregularities. If they found any, I would be taken out of there, and the state money would stop.

When I turned 13, the state visits had become fewer and farther between, and I knew it was only a matter of time. An incident occurred that I was blamed for, and I was sent upstairs. He started in, but I had always been a big kid and wrested the belt from his hands, giving him a taste of his own medicine and didn't stop until he swore that he'd leave all of us alone. He never touched us again, but after I'd left the house, running away at 16, I'd heard from my foster sister that he started up again on my younger foster brother, to the point where my brother finally couldn't stand it anymore and took his own life. I felt guilty about that for years, and it formed the place in my heart for people who couldn't defend themselves, the abused and the neglected.

I was worried about Shana and fairly certain that Paul was violent and abusive with Carla. It would only be a matter of time before he turned that anger on the little girl. Or much worse. Adding to it, I still couldn't shake the feeling that he was somehow connected to Earl's disappearance. I had no proof, but it nagged at me like a sore tooth.

My other concern was about going undercover. It wasn't in my wheelhouse and not the kind of thing I felt comfortable doing. These were dangerous people, and my trying to infiltrate the group seemed like a bad idea from every vantage point. Decker already knew who I was. I could maybe convince them that I believed in the movement but doubted they'd believe me right off the bat. There would be tests and gauntlets thrown down for me to run, and I wasn't keen on doing either.

"Get something for you, Tommy?"

It was Hanna, the other outside waitress. Hanna switched off between running an organic bakery across the way from Trinity and working there. She had a vague hippie vibe going and a great smile, unfortunately hidden by a Covid-19 mask.

"They still making you wear those? Gotta be hot, no?"

She nodded then rolled her eyes. "It's ridiculous but the state has all these rules we gotta follow until September. Can't wait."

"I hear ya. Yeah, just a Corona. No pun intended." She shot me a glance that told me it wasn't the first time she heard it. "And a menu."

She pointed to a sticker on the table that told me I had to point my camera at it to download a menu. I felt like I was a hundred years old. "Just the beer."

I called Carla again. I tried twice before I left the apartment, and no one answered either time. This time was no different. I decided to go back out there and see her in person.

Hanna brought the beer. I paid her, drank it down in a few minutes, and then walked back to the garage. The gun Mickey had sent with Jimmy was in the glove box, along with an extra box of shells he'd sent. I was hoping that I wouldn't need it but was extremely happy that I had it.

NINETEEN

The drive to Carla's house went quickly. I was getting used to it and enjoyed the road time, listening to the Tom Petty channel on Sirius radio in Mark's car. There still wasn't much traffic on the road.

As I pulled onto Carla's street, I noticed a familiar truck parked in front of her house and thought back to the guy who had tried to blackmail me back when I was getting a sandwich before returning to Veyo. I went past slowly and confirmed that it was the same truck, with the name Chris Lynde - Electrical Contractor stenciled on the side. I rolled past it, took a right at the next street, turned around in the first driveway I came to, then went back toward the house, pulling into a space about five houses down that had a clear view of the front of Carla's place.

I didn't have to wait long. Lynde came out of the house, followed closely by Paul. I watched them exchanging words, with Lynde nodding vigorously and Paul waving his finger to make a point. They shook hands, and Lynde got in his truck and sped by me. I pretended to be looking at my phone on the passenger seat.

Deciding to wait a few minutes before going to the door, I considered calling Carla first. It would be risky, with the possibility of Paul answering and making this into a confrontation. I sat there and watched, but a few minutes later the front door swung open and Paul came bounding out of the house, got into his car, and took off in the opposite direction from where I was parked.

I got out and walked down to the house. The yard looked different, and I couldn't put my finger on it at first. It wasn't until I walked up the stairs that it hit me. There were no toys in the yard or on the porch and no Big Wheel anywhere. I moved to the side of the porch and looked down toward the back of the house, but it was the same. Spotless.

I knocked on the door a few times, but no one answered. I went down the stairs and around to the side window of the kitchen where I saw Carla, sitting in the same chair she had been in when I first came to meet with her. She was bent over at the waist and was holding a towel to her head. I couldn't be sure, but she looked to be crying.

I didn't want to scare her, so I went around to the back of the house and knocked on the metal door there. It was unlocked and opened to a small foyer that looked like it was added on after the house was built. There was a washing machine and a dryer, with clothes scattered around on a side table and hanging on one of those portable racks used for air-drying clothes. There were no children's clothes that I could see.

Looking through the back door, I could see that Carla hadn't moved, so I knocked again, hard. She jumped, startled, and turned to look who it was with pure fear in her eyes. When she realized it was me, she sighed, relieved, then came to the door but didn't open it, yelling to me through the glass.

"Mr. Shore, you can't be here. Paul could come back any minute. You must leave. Now!"

I could see that her face was a mess, with bruises down the right side now. The last time I had been here, her left side had been puffy, but it had been covered up with makeup to hide it. These seemed recent, within the last few hours.

"Carla, please open up and let me come in. Or we can talk out here. I want to tell you about Earl and then get you to a safe place, away from here. Where's Shana?"

I could see her thinking it over and briefly got nervous about what her answer would be. She kept looking over her shoulder to the front room, sure that Paul was going to burst in any moment, see me, and do something horrendous to her. I needed to assure her that I would not let that happen.

"I won't let him hurt you. I saw that Chris Lynde was just here. I believe that Paul and Chris are part of a group of men here in town who are planning to do something illegal. Chris is a snake and probably told Paul something about me that Paul couldn't wait to tell the others in his group, so he won't be back for a while. In the meantime, we need you out of this house. Where's Shana?"

She looked at me and I could see her start to cry.

She unlocked the door, then sat back down in her kitchen chair. I opened it and went in, approaching her slowly. I wanted to express the urgency of getting her to come out of there with me.

"Can you get Shana and grab a few things that you'll need? I want to get you out of here and into a women's shelter as soon as possible. I believe Paul is going to hurt you so badly one of these days that there will be no turning back from it. And after you, he will turn on Shana. Guys like him aren't discerning about who they hurt. I've seen his kind before."

She was staring out the window again, much as she had done the first time I came here.

"Shana's no longer with me, no longer staying here. I had my other sister, Beth, come down from Windsor and take her away from here. I didn't think it was safe and couldn't protect her from him. I feel so much shame, Mr. Shore."

Her crying had intensified into sobs. I wasn't expecting that bit of news and needed more information. I spoke gently.

"Carla, please stop crying and tell me what happened. Did he do anything to Shana, hurt her or touch her in any way?"

She shook her head.

"No, but he's drinking again, and when he drinks, he gets angry--at the world, at everything. He hit me a few times recently over my calling you. I know he doesn't mean it, but I just can't take the chance. Like you said, he won't turn on her now, with Earl dead and all, but once he gets and spends the insurance money, who knows..."

It surprised me. She evidently knew about the insurance policy but had never mentioned it to me. I would ask her about it later.

"Carla, you can't ignore his behavior, it's dangerous. You also can't make excuses for him. His needs don't matter. You did the right thing with Shana before something happened. Now you need to focus on yourself. Please let me take you to a place you'll be safe?"

She looked at me, and I could see the weight of the world in her eyes. I waited. After a minute, she nodded, stood up, and went upstairs to pack a bag.

She came down 10 minutes later. In one hand, she had a large overnight bag that had clearly seen better days. In the other, a sweater-jacket. She saw me looking at it and knew what I was thinking.

"I know it's July and summer, but these places can be cold sometimes."

She had been through this routine before.

I took the bag from her hand, and we went out the back door. She locked it and went down the side of the house to the street. I wanted to be careful not to touch her, so I walked a few steps ahead rather than take her arm to guide her. I was aware she was looking around furtively the entire time. I threw the bag into my trunk, held the passenger door open for her until she got in, then walked around to the other side and got in. She started crying again, but her voice seemed stronger when she spoke.

"Thank you, Mr. Shore. I know this is the right thing to do."

I nodded. I was sure she didn't believe what she was telling me, but all I could do was try. I drove off back toward the Merritt Parkway.

I had googled a shelter called the Umbrella Center in New Haven while Carla was packing and saved the phone number and address. I auto-dialed it as I drove. When someone answered, I asked them to hold and handed the phone to Carla, telling her to give them her name and what the situation was. She told them what I suggested and then answered a series of yes-or-no questions, only stopping to ask me how long before we got there.

"Fifteen minutes, maybe twenty tops."

She repeated that and hung up. I looked over and asked if she was okay. She sighed and nodded.

I pulled up to the address and into the parking lot. The entrance was around the back, so I found a space as close to it as possible. The woman Carla spoke to had asked her to call the number again when we arrived to let them know we were there. I hit the autodial again and handed her the phone. She identified herself and was given instructions. We got out, and I took her bag from the trunk and waited for her to walk toward the steps leading inside. There were two women waiting there. One wore a security guard uniform, complete with holster and gun. The other was a young black woman with a clipboard. She opened the outer door, and Carla started up the stairs. I went to follow, but the woman with the clipboard stopped me.

"I'm sorry, just her."

Carla looked at me with a grimace, but I shook my head.

"It's gonna be okay. These folks will take care of you."

She leaned over and kissed my cheek. "Thank you."

I nodded, and she went inside.

The weight of the world.

I got back in my car and sat there, exhausted. The heat of the day had begun creeping up again, and the car was stifling, so I started it up and turned on the air full-blast. It didn't matter. I could barely breathe.

The case had fallen apart quickly and without much satisfaction. I should be thankful that I was able to get Carla out of what was clearly going to be a bad situation, but I couldn't bring myself to feel good about it. It was a short-term fix to a long-term problem. Once she was able to see how toxic her marriage was, the real work would have to start, and that was where one's resolve breaks down and most surrender to the easy way out. It would be a long road for her.

As for me, I had a decision to make. If I was honest with myself, there had never been a real case and now I had no client, and other than the hundred dollars Carla had forced me take, I wouldn't get paid.

The smart money was on Earl being dead. I was sure that Paul would be haranguing the insurance company for a payout immediately. They would stall him but eventually give in, especially if the local police deemed it a homicide. There was no body, but there was evidence enough that the only conclusion one could arrive at was that he had been tortured in that shack and then dumped somewhere, possibly in multiple places.

My involvement was iffy. I had been warned off and tacitly threatened. The person who had hired me had, in effect, fired me and was now in no position to ask me to continue. She had no means to pay me, and her husband wanted me to go away.

Something I'd read or heard kept coming back to me: that the farthest distance in the world was between how it is and how you thought it was going to be.

A hard lesson to learn and an even harder one to accept.

PART 2

TWENTY

Three weeks had passed since I dropped Carla off at the shelter and decided to walk away from the case. At first, the shelter made it difficult to stay in touch with her by not allowing her many phone calls and by imposing stringent rules that needed to be adhered to absolutely. She had a hard time adjusting to being there. The first time we spoke, there was a litany of complaints about the food, about her personal things that had gone missing, and about the attitudes of the people who worked there. I mostly agreed with her on that last point and wasn't sure that the "tough love" approach was the way to go with someone who was as fragile as she seemed to be.

The second time we spoke, it was a very different Carla, one who had clearly given in and given up. During the call, it felt like I had to buy every word. When she mumbled something about "thinking of going back home," I tried to gently remind her how dangerous that would be. Her response was clear:

"I'd rather die there than live here. There's no life for me in this place."

My attempt to reassure her that it would only be temporary and that things would get better fell on deaf ears. I wasn't sure I believed it myself. We hung up with me promising that I would call her back in a few days.

After I'd brought her there, I had gone straight home and called Moreland to tell him I was out. He got angry and tried hard to change my mind, appealing to my "duty as a citizen." I told him my duty didn't include getting myself killed and, after 10 minutes of badgering, he hung up, slamming the phone in my ear. I felt bad for about two minutes, then realized I was just hungry. I took the car to the Glenwood Drive-In in Hamden for a hot dog and an order of onion rings, after which I brought the car I'd borrowed back to my friend's house. I called a Lyft to get home from there and stayed holed up inside my apartment for the next four days, only venturing out to the bodega across the street to get cereal or bread.

I doubled down on my ads in the *New Haven Register*, but the phone still didn't ring much. People were still just getting back to work, and money was tight everywhere. I thought there'd be an influx of spouses taking off and needing to be found, but that wasn't the case, so I started looking in the want-ads for part-time work and using the online services. Most of what was available was delivering food for local restaurants. Without a car, it probably wasn't an option.

I cut down a little on my drinking for a while. Like most bars, the Owl had changed dramatically after the virus, and I had stopped going. Once people could be let inside, strict protocols were imposed by the state, and owners needed to comply or be fined or shut down.

The Owl complied more than most. A plastic divider was hung between the bar and the six stools in front of it, making it feel sterile sitting there. You could sit at a table but had to reserve it by phone, and if it was reserved for a later time, you had to get up and leave when that person or persons showed up. They made customers wear masks on the way in, on the way out, and if you wanted to use the restroom, you needed to get permission from the bartender. Guess that made him the "head" bartender.

Many of the regular staff didn't return. There was no one working there that I knew and had grown friendly with over the years since I'd been drinking there. No one really knew me at all. I went in once after customers were being let inside and could feel the stares and furtive glances. I sat at a table and ordered a beer but got no interaction at all from the waitress until she brought it back to me and asked me to pay my check. I balked a little.

"I usually run a tab and pay when I leave."

She grimaced and looked angry.

"We don't do that anymore. It's a pay-as-you-go bar now. No cash."

I shrugged and gave her my credit card, downing the entire beer before she came back with the receipt for me to sign. I signed it, left her a buck tip, and hadn't gone back since.

Trinity was a different story. It had changed even from the last time I was there, post-virus. The city started enforcing the rules diligently, and an owner could now lose their license. The actual bar at Trinity was open but now only on the one side. They obeyed the social distancing edicts but didn't ask for reservations and never put up the partitions. Still, it wasn't the same, and I wasn't sure it ever would be. When I drank, I drank at home.

It was late one night when a call came in on the landline. I was already well into my third Jameson of the night. It was Carla, calling from her house in Wallingford.

"Mr. Shore, it's Carla Vitter. I just wanted to call and tell you that I left the shelter and that I'm back home with Paul."

I listened. The booze had mellowed me, and I didn't want to lose that feeling by letting anger creep in.

"Okay."

"I don't want you to be angry with me, but you know how much I hated being in that place. I couldn't stay there another minute. I called Paul and we talked. He said that he's a changed man and told me that it was going to be different with him. He started back going to AA meetings and he's also getting help dealing with his issues. I believe him."

She sounded like she was trying to convince herself as much as me. Enough time had passed, and I had begun to distance myself from the case, such as it was. Still, her litany of excuses triggered something inside me, and I had to catch myself before I got mad and started to argue with her.

"Carla, I completely understand. It's your life. You need to do what you feel is right for you. Is Shana back living with you?"

There was a hesitation. I'd hit on a sore point. When she spoke, I could hear the catch in her voice.

"Not yet...she's still with my sister. We're going to get her tomorrow. She needs to be in a home where she's loved, be with people who want her."

Sure. Especially if there's a possibility of her getting an insurance windfall from the death of her father that would need adult oversight.

"Have the Wallingford police contacted you about Earl? Have there been further developments? I read in the paper that they found his car in that pond but not that they'd found him."

More hesitation. I considered the possibility that Paul was probably standing close by, orchestrating the entire conversation. She didn't want to say anything that would anger him. It was a snapshot of the rest of her life, of living on pins and needles.

"Well, that detective who came by to question us, Decker, he came by again and told us that the police believe he's dead. He said they've found evidence that corroborates it."

That surprised me.

"They found a body?"

"No, but he said they were still looking. Evidently, they found blood in the car and think there was foul play."

I was going to ask her a few more questions, but I could hear noises in the background, and the next thing I heard was her brusquely thanking me for my help, then saying goodbye and hanging up. I stared at the phone for a few seconds, then set it back down in its cradle. I finished my drink and poured another. I needed to sleep, but my mind was racing now.

The last one actually did the trick. I went off for what seemed like a few hours but awoke when I heard the vibration from my cell phone hitting the sides of the ashtray next to my chair where I'd left it. I picked it up and looked at the information but didn't recognize the number. I was still a little drunk and groggy, but I answered anyway.

"Tommy Shore."

"Tom? John Moreland, state police. Can you talk?"

I looked at the clock on the stove. 8:43. I had been out for over 10 hours.

"Well, I'm half asleep and still a little drunk from last night. What do you need?"

"I need to talk to you. In person. In an official capacity. When would you be available?"

An official capacity. Interesting...in the Chinese curse sort of way.

"Okay. Give me an hour, then come over. You know the address."

He agreed and hung up. I got up, took a shower, got dressed, made a pot of coffee, put away the glasses and the booze from the night before, and then tried to make the place vaguely presentable.

I had a weird gut feeling that I was about to hear something that was going to change things.

TWENTY-ONE

Moreland showed up exactly an hour after he called. It made me think he'd been waiting outside when he made the phone call and had been killing time since then until I was ready.

I opened the door when he knocked, and he entered before I could invite him in.

"Sure, why not, come on in."

He was dressed more casually this time. He still had on an expensive blazer but wore a polo shirt under it. I could see a hint of a logo. He was so gung-ho that I was betting it probably said "State Police." The pants had a sharp crease, but he wore topsiders with white socks. The cliché of it amused me.

"Staties letting you dress sporty these days, John?"

He looked confused at first, then looked down at what he had on. He shook his head, scowled, then looked back to me.

"Shore, Earl Scosa's dead, confirmed. His body was discovered a few days ago, not far from the pond where his car had been found. He was left in the woods, and the animals had been at it pretty good, but we were still able to get a positive ID. We could tell that he had been worked over. The M.E. says cause of death was a brain bleed from trauma, possibly a couple of blows to the head with a blunt object. A bat or a hammer."

He was waiting for a reaction from me as he ticked this information off, and when it didn't come, the scowl grew even more pronounced.

"What, you're not surprised? You already figured him for dead?"

I scowled back at him.

"Look. I told you I was there, at the spot where they found the car. I got a good look inside the shack and could see that something nasty had happened there. I could smell blood. Part of me thought it might be a hunting shack, but when I saw inside, there was stuff in there that told me it was clearly used for something other than hunting. Torture. Based on the amount of blood that was there, I doubt anyone could have lived after that."

I paused to catch my breath.

"I also told you that I called it in to a local reporter, counting on him to call the cops. Which he did. They got there in record time, like they knew exactly where they were going. Decker showed up, too. When no one called for an ambulance or a medical examiner, I figured there was no body in the car. I wasn't sure, so I went to see the reporter, to see if he had any more info. He half-assed warned me off of this, telling me that Decker was a piece of work and that these small-town cops were dangerous, that I needed to be careful. He was supposed to get back to me with more information, but he never did. I figured it was a dead end. The story that ran was all he had."

Moreland sat down on the couch. He was shaking his head. I needed liquid.

"You want something to drink? Water, coffee? I'm gonna get some."

He shook his head, and I went to the counter and poured a cup for myself. I was aware he was watching me closely, waiting. I came back to where he was and sat facing him in my chair.

"My client, Carla Vitter, called me right after that and told me that I was no longer on the case. I know that her husband made her fire me. It was clear from the jump that he didn't want me around. I'd had suspicions that there was domestic abuse going on there but didn't know the extent of it. I was sure Carla was a victim but also worried about Scosa's little girl that she was watching. The husband, Paul, is a piece of work, a miserable asshole with no redeeming factors, as far as I can tell. Says he's sober, but the one time I met him I could smell booze on him from four feet away. I'm also fairly sure that he's involved with The Knights of the Message."

Moreland had been taking notes on a small pad, but his head snapped up at the mention of the Knights.

"How do you know that?"

"I was approached by this idiot guy, Chris Lynde. He's an electrician in Wallingford. He's also a moron. He offered to get me information on where Earl was in exchange for cash. At first, I thought it was a shakedown, but now I'm convinced he was just trying to find out what my involvement was and how much I knew. He said he was a running buddy with Scosa, that they both worked for Veyo, but I think that was a front, too.

After you told me that Scosa was trying to infiltrate the group, I started thinking about Lynde getting in my face. It was too much of a coincidence, too pat. When I went to check in on Carla, Lynde's truck was parked in front. I watched for a while, Lynde and Paul Vitter came out, exchanged some words, and Lynde left. Vitter came out a minute later, and he took off as well. My guess is he went to Decker to tell him what Lynde told him about me. So, no, I'm not surprised Scosa's dead."

Moreland continued scowling. I was going to warn him that his face might get stuck like that, but it didn't seem like he was in the mood for my sense of humor. He looked at his notes before he spoke.

"Vitter's definitely a person of interest. We think he may be high up in the Knight's organization. You said, 'your guess'? You don't know for sure?"

I shook my head.

"I didn't follow either one. I went inside the house to check on my ex-client and found her in pretty rough shape. I was able to get her to leave and got her into a women's shelter. She didn't last long there and called me last night to tell me that she had gone back home to Paul. The little girl is staying with Carla's sister up north and isn't back with them yet."

He sat back and looked at me, deciding how much he wanted to tell me.

"Look, Shore, here's the thing. The investigation has stalled. Losing Scosa had a major impact and everything's ground to a standstill."

It was my turn to scowl.

"Don't ya just hate how torture and murder can do that?"

If Moreland was angry, he didn't show it. Instead, he pulled an envelope out of his pocket and handed it to me. I looked at it like he'd given me a dead mouse.

"What's this?"

He nodded his chin at me.

"It's a check. I went to my superiors, and we discussed possible scenarios. Told them about the insurance payoff on Scosa and how Paul Vitter would have access to the money. They said they would lock that down until it could be investigated. I also suggested that we might enlist your help by getting you paid. I thought things might be getting tight, after you intimated that you probably wouldn't be getting any money from this."

I could feel my face redden. They thought they had me in a bind and that I would jump at the chance to make a few bucks. I was embarrassed that they weren't wrong. I opened the envelope and there was a check in it for twenty-five hundred dollars. I laughed.

"Tax-payer dollars hard at work, eh?"

"Shore, Scosa was one of our own. Undercover is risky business, but we can't let this go, we've come too far. You have a way of getting into places that we can't get into right now. They're going to be suspicious of anyone new. This is real money, and all you have to do to earn it is to find out what you can. I don't care how you do it. Tell them whatever you need to. Say you found out that he was working for us and convince them that your beliefs parallel theirs. We're good with whichever way you want to play it...as long as we get enough to take these bastards down. They're going to do something, and we want to be there before they do."

I had my head down, massaging my temples with my right hand while I thought it over. A major headache had come on, partly from being hungover but mostly from what he was asking me to do. This felt extremely dangerous, but I needed the cash. I looked up and nodded.

"Okay, I'll get involved but here's the deal. I do it my way, and you get whatever I come up with. I don't check in on a regular basis and we don't meet here anymore. I'll let you know when I have something, and we can figure out a place to meet. No exceptions. My way, all the way. Comprende?"

Moreland looked at me, nodded, then got up and started for the door. He paused with his hand on the doorknob and turned back to me.

"I know it's useless to say this to you but be careful. The reporter was right, these people don't play around. That's why we need to end them, and quickly."

It was my turn to nod. I fought the urge to salute. Somehow, it didn't seem appropriate.

TWENTY-TWO

I decided to go back out to Wallingford to see if I could find and talk to Chris Lynde. I wasn't sure it would take me anywhere, but he had shown up twice unexpectedly since this thing started. It was the only lead I had, and tentative as it was, I needed to follow it.

During the last three weeks, there hadn't been much going on, but one day a package was left at my door. I never saw the delivery person and was skeptical at first. While I was looking at the box on my kitchen table, the phone rang and it was Jimmy, Mickey's driver.

"Tommy, Jimmy. He wanted me to let you know that the box that was left was from him, so it's safe to open. Some of the items you requested are in there." The line went dead before I could say anything.

I took out a box cutter and opened it up. Inside was a beautifully weighted sap, a set of brass knuckles, a box of hollow-point bullets for the .38 Jimmy had given me before, and two small stun guns. I laughed. If nothing else, Mickey was thorough.

I put everything into an old canvas grip bag, threw

in two sets of plastic handcuffs and the gun, then called Hertz and ordered a black VW Jetta. I poured some of the coffee I'd made into a thermos and left, grabbing an egg and cheese sandwich on the walk down to the rental place.

I looked up an address for Lynde. His electrical business was on Main Street, and Google maps showed it to be a small storefront with an old sign in what looked to be a fairly dilapidated building. Once I had the car, I programmed the address into Waze and headed out there.

I was just past North Haven when my cell phone buzzed. It was Carla.

"Mr. Shore? Tommy?" She was whispering.

'Yep, it's me. What's up?" I was still annoyed with her but was trying to keep it out of my voice.

"Tommy, I need to warn you. I feel I owe you that, for everything you've done for me, trying to help me and all. Paul's been making threats about you. He claims you're the reason he can't get the insurance money on Earl, that you put a bug in somebody's ear who's holding it up. He says they're stalling him. He's very angry."

I couldn't tell if she was actually afraid or if, once again, Paul put her up to this.

"Carla, is he standing right there? Were you supposed to try to get me to talk to somebody, take back what I said about him? Just say yes or no."

There was a pause and then softly, "Yes."

"Put him on."

There was a shuffling sound and some muted conversation, then Paul got on.

"What do you want, Shore? I know you've been

talking shit about me, that you're the monkey wrench in this whole deal. You're one of the reasons keeping us from getting the money we need to take care of Earl's little girl. People like you."

He was spitting the words out, and the hate in his voice came through loud and clear. I kept my voice level, stifling the bile I felt.

"You know who's gonna end you, Vitter? People like me. You're quite the tough guy when it comes to hitting women, but I'm happy to meet you somewhere to discuss just how tough you are. Just the two of us, without your cadre of sheet wearers."

He hung up. Nice job, Thomas, winning hearts and minds. I got nervous for a second that he might take it out on Carla, but I doubted he would chance that before he had custody of Shana and access to the insurance cash. He would need to show a unified front with her, or someone might actually question the bruises on his wife's face.

I got to Lynde's place twenty minutes later and parked across the street, finding a space in the lot of a small strip mall. There was a pizza place, a dry cleaner, and an insurance agency and a good amount of traffic. By backing into a spot near the street, I could easily watch Lynde's place. It was as rundown as it appeared on the computer. There looked to be an old console television in the front window, along with a neon sign flickering LYNDE ELECTRICS on and off, hanging from some wires. The window was caked with so much dirt and dust that I couldn't read the sign that was inside the window, at least not from where I sat. Most likely, it was his hours of operation.

On the side of the building toward the back, I could

see Lynde's truck, so I knew he was in there. I decided to wait a bit to see if anyone else came along and joined him inside.

When twenty minutes had passed and no one else approached, I got out and crossed the street, staying as close as possible to the side of the building. I brought along the sap, a set of plastic cuffs, and the brass knuckles out of the bag, just in case.

I tried the door handle and it turned easily, left unlocked. Stupidity born of arrogance. I moved inside and locked it from within.

The door opened to a large back room, filled with shelving, all holding boxes of electrical parts, fuses, wires, tools, and other crap. There was dust on everything.

I sidled my way quietly towards the front of the place, keeping as close to the shelves as possible without disturbing anything that was sticking out from them. When I got closer to the door leading out to the storefront, I heard a noise, a muted zap of something being fused together. I peered around the last shelf and saw Lynde, hunched over a workbench, soldering.

The socket wrench was sitting in one of the boxes near me and I quietly pulled it out. Moving as slowly as possible, I came up behind Lynde, jammed the bottom of the wrench into the small of his back, and whispered, "Put the soldering gun down and do not turn around." He froze and took his finger off the soldering gun's trigger. It was completely quiet until he finally spoke.

"How'd you get in here?"

I shook my head and said, "You left the door unlocked, moron."

Lynde had straightened upright but hadn't turned

around. I had the wrench firmly pressed against his spine and knew he couldn't be sure it wasn't a gun. The weighted sap was in my left hand in case he tried anything.

"Whatcha making?" I asked him in a mocking way, peering over his shoulder at the workbench. There was everything there that I imagined one would need to fashion a homemade shrapnel bomb: two large boxes of nails, pipe tubing, a couple of rolls of masking tape, timing devices, and three containers of Pyrodex, a gunpowder substitute. There was also a container of something called Amatex. I was betting that was the explosive.

"You learn how to do all this shit in shop class or on YouTube?"

Lynde threw his head back hard, trying to hit me in the face. Probably saw it in some low budget British crime movie. I jerked back in time and brought the sap around and connected it with the side of his temple, hard. He crumbled to the floor immediately, out cold.

I took out my phone and snapped pictures of all the materials on the desk, then texted them to Moreland. A response came back within seconds, asking me for a location. I texted the address back and told him to use the back door. His message back to me said to hang tight, that they'd be there in a few minutes. I sent a thumbs-up emoji and clicked off. Gotta love technology.

Pulling out the plastic cuffs, I pushed Lynde onto his stomach and pulled his hands hard behind him, fitting the cuffs over his wrists and pulling the tie as tight as I could. He groaned a little but was still out. His head would be pounding later.

I went to the back door and unlocked it, then came back and found an old wooden desk chair to sit on while I waited, watching Lynde as he started to come around on the floor. He groaned again but stayed out.

A few minutes later, I heard the door open and Moreland whisper-yell my name.

"Back here."

He came down the aisle and stopped when he saw Lynde on the floor.

"Jeez, you didn't kill him, did ya?"

I couldn't tell if he was serious or if this passed for state police humor.

"No, he's just out cold from a sap to the head."

Moreland winced. "Ow, that's gotta hurt. Maybe you need to be out of here before he comes around. We'll pack up all this stuff and take it and him in."

As he said it, another guy came in, carrying four folded boxes that had EVIDENCE printed on the side and a masking tape gun. I assumed he was a statie as well, working for Moreland. He had the haircut and the posture. He quickly started taping the boxes together, taking photos of the material, and then putting it all into the boxes.

I looked back at Moreland and nodded.

I told him, "I'll call you later," then cautiously went out the back door and walked briskly across the street to my car. I pulled out from the lot and headed towards Carla's house. I hoped to get some information from Lynde about Paul, but that game plan changed abruptly when I saw the bomb stuff. Hopefully, Moreland could get something concrete and usable out of him.

TWENTY-THREE

It was a short ride to Carla's from Lynde's joint. I was getting used to the side streets and the shortcuts and was now able to come down to a street where I could stay out of sight but still keep watch on the house. I parked and waited. No one came in or out. A few cars went by the house, but no one stopped.

After a half hour or so, I remembered the thermos of coffee and reached into the back seat to grab it. When I turned back around, I noticed that one of the cars, a green Chevy Impala that had passed by before, was passing again. It slowed down in front of Vitter's house, then kept going around the corner. I slumped down in my seat and waited some more. Another five minutes passed, then the same car came around for a third time. The front door of the house swung open, and Paul came bounding out, taking the steps in two strides and hurriedly getting into the front passenger seat. The Connecticut license plate was so caked with dirt that I could only make out the last three letters, MLN. It was hard to tell who was in the car but I thought there might have been at least one other guy sitting in the back seat. Before Vitter even shut his door, they had begun to roll out.

I gave it a few seconds and then followed. There weren't many cars out at this time of day so I needed to be careful, hanging back to keep from being spotted. When they finally got off the side streets and onto the main drag, I was able to close some of the distance. I tailed them up Main Street until they turned into the Super Walmart parking lot and backed into a space that was furthest from the main entrance yet allowed them to watch the doors. I jockeyed to a space about five rows away, closer to the front but with a clear view of the Impala.

Fifteen minutes went by before there was any movement, then the car began to roll forward. I watched as they crept slowly up the aisle towards the entrance, then swung the car around and stopped in front, as if they were picking up someone who had been shopping in the store. They were only there about 30 seconds when a guy came out, walked briskly to the Chevy, and got into the back seat on the driver's side. The driver pulled the car out of the parking lot, heading towards the back entrance and began picking up speed. I followed them out the back driveway, keeping a car between us. When they got to the side street exit, they turned left and went back towards Route 5, then turned right. I hung back until there was a second car between us, then followed them until they turned onto another side road a few miles down from where we'd been.

The strip mall they turned into looked familiar to me, and it only took a few seconds to realize that it was the same plaza where the barbecue place had been, where Jimmy and I had gone to eat after finding the car. The Impala headed towards the restaurant but then veered off towards the opposite corner of the mall, stopping at a storefront with a banner proclaiming VETERANS FOR A FREE AMERICA. On either side of that banner was an American flag and hanging next to it was a Gadsden flag, ominous in black with a coiled rattlesnake and the words DON'T TREAD ON ME stitched into it. I had read that it was originally designed by Christopher Gadsden, a brigadier general in the Continental Army for use against the British. Now it was being used as one of the key symbols by second-amendment zealots and Tea Partyers. I had a feeling I was in the right place.

I used my phone to take photos at Walmart of the guy getting into the car, and I now used it to get a few more of the four men as they got out and went in to the storefront. I also got pictures of the banner and the flags. My viewpoint from near the barbecue joint was unobstructed, and I wasn't worried about being spotted. My car looked like it could belong to any other patron eating there.

I attached everything to an email, sent it to Moreland, texted him that it would be coming through, then waited for a response. I had a fleeting thought of how different life would have been if Lew Archer or Philip Marlowe had been able to use this kind of technology back in the day. Different, not necessarily better.

Moreland's response came back immediately: "Back off immediately and leave the area." He would explain to me later. I closed the text and quickly drove out of the lot, getting back onto the parkway heading home. He called a few minutes later. I hit the button for the speaker phone, and he didn't wait for me to say hello.

"Shore, no one saw you, right? Please tell me no one saw you."

I was confused by the panic in his voice. "No one saw me or knew I was there. They picked up Vitter at home, I followed them to the Walmart, another guy came out of there and got in, and I followed them to the place I texted you about. End of story. What's this about, what's the problem?"

There was a pause, then, "Where are you now, Shore?"

"Heading back to New Haven, on the Merritt. Not sure what I should do next."

"Okay, go home and wait for me to contact you with a place where we can meet. I'd come to you again, but you told me not to. I agree, we should change up locations, in case someone's watching. Might be paranoid but you can't be too careful. Good?"

I felt myself getting angry.

"No. It's not good. Why would someone be watching me? As far as anyone knows, I'm off the case and no longer an issue for these guys. What aren't you telling me? Do I need to watch my back?"

Moreland picked up on my anger and tried to calm me down.

"Tommy, relax. I'm just being careful. It's never a bad idea to play it safe, cover all the bases. Look, I'll just come to you, okay? It's easier. I can be at your apartment in two hours. Okay?"

Against my better judgment, I agreed, then hung up. I was already breaking my own rules.

By the time I walked into my apartment, I had

worked myself up into a serious froth. I was pissed at Vitter, I was disappointed with Carla, and I was mad at the cops, at Lynde, and especially at Moreland...but couldn't really decide where to direct it. Which meant I was mostly angry at myself. If I take the money from Moreland, he held the reins. I would be bought and paid for. It shouldn't be any different than taking money from clients, but somehow it felt different. I could feel my temples throb.

I never knew what to do with myself when I got in this state of mind. In the old days, I would have called up Reilly, and we'd get trashed. But that bridge had been crossed and blown up, its parts washed downstream.

No, I had to do something physical, work it out of my system. I didn't have enough time to head to the gun range in Hamden, so I opted for a quick run. I had been getting lazy and soft during the isolation and felt like I'd put on weight. Maybe not the usual "Covid-19 pounds" the pundits were yammering about but at least five. I had been working the heavy bag I'd gotten out of my closet and hung up in the living room, but running would help me start toward getting rid of the stuff around my gut.

I changed into some sweats and running shoes and headed out the side entrance, going down toward Temple Street to Crown and then down toward State Street and over to the train station. By the time I reached there, I had built up a good sweat. I was hot and I was thirsty, so I stopped inside the station and went to the snack shop to grab a water. The woman behind the counter grimaced at how wet I was, and I wasn't sure she was going to take the two dollars I brought with me. She was wearing a mask and looked at the cash like it was not of this planet. I dropped it on top of some newspapers, told her to keep the change, and then headed back out.

I ran down State until I came to the Elm City Market, then headed up Chapel, running the last block full out, and then cooled down by walking from the corner into my building. I was soaked but felt better. Much of the tension had dissipated.

I took a shower when I got in and was toweling off when I heard the knock at the door. Throwing some clothes on, I looked around and spotted the bag with the goodies from Mickey. I tossed it under the sink, then opened the door.

Moreland came in quickly, without invitation, as he had done the last two times. He looked at my wet hair, t-shirt, shorts, and bare feet and scoffed.

"Nice to be self-employed, eh?"

He sat down in his usual spot on the couch and put a folder I hadn't noticed down on the coffee table. He opened it and ruffled through the pages until he came to some more photographs.

I looked at him and walked over to the kitchen island where I had left his uncashed check under an ashtray. I picked it up and walked over to the coffee table, tossing the envelope so it landed on his folder.

"I'm out. This bullshit isn't worth it. Get these guys on your own."

I could see he was surprised by that. He put his hands up in a mock surrender.

"Hey, man, settle down. Really. I'm kidding. Just giving you a little shit. We still need you to help us.

Look, let me tell you what's going on, and then if you want me to go, I'll go, no questions asked. Deal?"

My curiosity got the better of me. I glanced quickly at the pile of bills on the counter when I'd picked up the check and was now vacillating between indignation and survival mode.

"Go ahead."

"Look, you may have earned out that cash already. We got a fair amount of information from Lynde. Not the sharpest knife in the drawer, right? He basically spilled his guts after we sweated him a few hours."

As I listened, it occurred to me that Moreland was an old-time movie fan, down to the antiquated lingo. Then he handed me the stack of photos. It was basically the same as the ones he had shown me before, a bunch of guys having a meeting somewhere. I said as much.

"What is it I'm supposed to be looking at? This looks exactly like the last bunch you showed me, with Decker leading the charge."

He got up and came over to where I was standing at the counter.

"No, look closer. Look at the board behind Decker, at the front of the room. There's a list there."

I squinted hard until the list of names came into focus. Then I saw it. Behind Decker was a white board where they had listed most of the major government buildings--the Capitol building, the State Senate, the Connecticut Supreme Court building, the Governor's Residence. And not just Hartford. New Haven's Superior Courthouse was also on the list. Targets.

I handed the photographs back to him. "Jesus."

"Yessir. Mary and Joseph, too. These guys mean business. Fortunately, as of right now, we don't think they have the know-how to construct anything that could do the major damage they want. That moron you led us to today, with his home-made shrapnel pipe bombs? He's the only one that seems to know how to make anything resembling munitions. Don't get me wrong, what he was making would make a lot of noise and ruin some lives...but the real danger is the signal that setting one of those things off would send to other crazies out there who *do* know how to make something more powerful and are just itching for a group that would appreciate their particular talent."

I could feel the throbbing around my temples intensify as I listened to him.

"I don't get this. What are they trying to prove? Is it political or is this totally about hate?"

Moreland sat back down.

"It's about a lot of things. At the base of it, it's hate of different races, different religions, and different ideology. Pure and simple. On another level, there's this cockamamie movement toward smaller government...fewer taxes, less restrictions and regulations. That kind of thing, I guess, which, to me, comes back to stupidity and ignorance."

I shook my head as he continued, leaning forward and lowering his voice conspiratorially.

"I wanted you to leave where you were today because I already have somebody deep undercover there. I can't risk making these guys paranoid because, if they spotted you in the area, who knows how'd they react. My guy's hanging on by a thread as it is, and it wouldn't take much to break that thread. Especially after Scosa got found out."

The weight of what he was saying was making me

even more tired. I wanted to go somewhere and drink. Or sit alone in my easy chair, crank up the air conditioning, and pour my own booze until I passed out.

"What do you want me to do, John? Giving you Lynde obviously didn't clear my slate."

He looked at me for a minute, then down at the folder he'd brought. I couldn't tell what he was thinking.

"Tommy, I really just need you to just hang tight right now. I'll speak to my superiors and see what the right plan of action should be. Once we have that, I'll know what to do. It may be nothing and we're square. But if they want you to do something more, I'll let you know that. We're a team and you're an important part of it. This needs to be surgical. Can you do that, can you stay put until we talk again?"

He spoke these words to me in a soothing voice, almost monotone. Trying to calm me down. Team. When did I become part of a team? I thought about it for a few seconds, sighed, and nodded. He got up, smiled at me, nodded goodbye, and then walked out of the apartment. As always, it was so abrupt, I laughed out loud.

I looked back at the coffee table. He had left the check.

TWENTY-FOUR

Once again, I found myself having to lay low and wait things out. Neither of those was a strong aspect of my character. The first two days, I took to walking around the city a couple of times a day. At first, it felt good to revisit the places I'd grown to love, the restaurants and bars and coffee shops and clubs that made up the heart of life in New Haven. However, by the third day, the subtle changes that had occurred during the pandemic became much more noticeable to me.Most places continued to stay empty inside. Those that had space for outside dining or activity utilized the city ordinance that allowed them to rent parking spaces and erect makeshift patios, cordoned off by velvet ropes or over-sized plant boxes. Not much protection from cars that could still use the street to drive by.

The mood of the people sitting outside at these places seemed to be tentative at best. The furtive glances that I had been aware of previously now seemed to take hold in a much more pronounced way. The monkey cage come to life. Everyone was hyperaware and on constant lookout for proper social distancing, masks, and respect for space from staff and from other patrons.

By day four, I decided to forego my morning walks and opted to stay in, drink coffee, and read the *New Haven Register*. It wasn't a great paper, but it kept me up on local events and the surrounding towns. I neglected this particular pleasure during my second voluntary isolation, and it felt good getting back to it.

After first checking for my ad near the barely existent sports page (which had become even smaller), I turned to the obituary page, smiling as I remembered that this section had been my foster mother's favorite part of the paper, her first go-to at the breakfast table. She would make various noises in her throat if she spotted someone she knew, even if the acquaintance was only slight. When I would ask about it, she'd click her tongue and say, "Never you mind. You'll be looking on your own someday." She was right on the money.

I scanned the rest of the names and looked at the pictures but didn't recognize anyone. I turned back to the front page and scanned that quickly, turning next to the police log, a section that was dedicated to all the lowlifes and scumbags who had been arrested recently in the area. Occasionally, I found it to be a place of names for possible clients, people who might need someone to look for evidence surrounding their particular case. More often than not, it was a source of great humor for me, as I read about some of the more ridiculous ways that people found to break the law.

Today was different. As soon as I focused on the section, a familiar name jumped out: Paul Vitter.

He had been arrested for domestic violence, and his

bail had been set at fifty thousand dollars. The bond, five thousand dollars, had been posted using funds that were put up by the Veterans for a Free America. There was no mention of Carla.

I called Carla's house immediately but hung up after the first ring. If he was there and heard it was me, it would set him off. Even more than that, it would set me off if he answered the phone. It meant she took him back yet again.

I knew I couldn't chance going out there. If I saw him, my lesser angels would take over, and I would be the one needing to post bail. I racked my brain for what to do.

I was feeling a weird combination of guilt, anger, and frustration, none of which made sense. I kept telling myself that I tried to help her, but she chose to return to him and this was the result. The phrase "I warned you" kept running through my brain, but it was a useless thought. I couldn't shake the feeling that, even as I saw this coming, I didn't warn her persistently enough. I knew on the logical side of my brain that I did what I could, but the emotional side kept telling me that I should have kept at it until I convinced her to leave. Instead, the booze enabled me to let it pass when she first called to tell me that she was back home.

Shaking off the guilt, I took out my note pad and started going through it to see if anything jumped out that might give me a direction to go in. I was in a tailspin and needed to do something.

I had jotted a note that she had a sister who lived in Windsor and that Shana was staying there. Her sister's name was Beth, but I didn't have a maiden name or a married name, so it was useless. It made me realize that

I didn't know where the little girl was, whether she had come back to Carla's as had been mentioned was going to happen, or if she was still living with her other aunt. If she had been brought back to Carla before the incident occurred, she was most likely with DCS now, lost somewhere in the system.

The possibility that Paul did enough damage to hospitalize her occurred to me, and the only hospital I knew of with an ER local to Wallingford was Mid-State Medical Center in Meriden. I decided to call them on the off-chance they might tell me if Carla was admitted there. It was a long shot, but I didn't have much else go on.

After getting passed from one desk to another, I finally got an admissions official who agreed to give me a yes-or-no answer to my mentioning a name and confirmed that Carla was there. I got dressed as quickly as possible, got the car, and headed out.

The hospital was off I-91, on the main road that ran all the way from downtown through the suburbs. It was easy enough to find, and I pulled into the parking lot less than 30 minutes after leaving the garage at my apartment.

I drove around the lot a few times, trying to see if I could spot Vitter's van, then parked and watched the entrance. After 10 minutes had gone by and I thought it was safe, I got out and walked inside.

There was a checkpoint set up for the litany of Covid-19 questions. "Have you been out of the country or state?," "Have you flown?," "Have you been feverish or felt any of the symptoms?" Those kinds of questions. After answering no to them all, you were asked to step in front of a device that looked like an iPhone sitting on a stand that took your temperature. Mine came up as 97.5. Not bad, coming out of the air-conditioned car. The nurse directed me toward the reception desk, where a woman in a hijab was sitting, watching me closely and probably wondering what fresh hell I would bring. I gave her my biggest smile and asked to see Carla Vitter. She smiled back and tapped the name into the computer.

"Are you family?"

She looked directly at me and waited.

"Yes Ma'am. I'm a cousin."

It was hard to tell if she believed me or if she was deciding on whether to alert security.

"I'm sorry, but the hospital only allows visitation from immediate family, spouses, children or parents."

I maintained my smile, tightening it up a bit so I didn't look like a complete idiot.

"Understood. It's just that I came all the way down from Maine to see her--we were really close as kids--and it would just be awful to have come all that way and not be able to see and say hello to my favorite cousin. Family is so important, don't you agree?"

There was a slight arch to one of her eyebrows, but she continued smiling back and told me to wait where I was, getting up and going into one of the offices that was behind her. She returned a minute later and said the director wanted to speak to me, gesturing for me to go into the office that she had come out of. I nodded, walked around the desk, and went in.

Standing behind a large wooden desk was a small woman, maybe five feet tall. She had close-cropped blond hair, largish pink glasses and was wearing a light blue polo shirt with the name of the hospital on it and a white doctor's jacket over it. Her name tag read ANGELA BODINE. She looked to be a good twenty pounds overweight, but there was a sturdiness to her, like the weight might actually be muscle. I was surprised. She didn't seem like a typical bureaucrat, and unlike the woman at the desk, she wasn't smiling. Without saying anything, she used her hand to indicate that I should sit down on the chair in front of her desk, then sat down herself. I realized she must be the person I spoke to on the phone. There was a folder on the desk in front of her that she must have been going through before I got here. She opened it up again and continued to go through it. She looked up after a minute and addressed me.

"Are you Thomas Shore?"

Surprised again. My mind raced with the possible ways of how she could know that. For a second, I thought she might have been warned by Decker but dismissed it quickly. Didn't make any sense. I decided to come clean.

"That's me, but you can call me Tommy."

She nodded and continued looking through the folder, then opened a drawer and tossed it in there, looking directly at me.

"I'm Angela Bodine. You can call me Mrs. Bodine. I can take you to see Ms. Vitter. She's been here a few days now. When she first came in, she went in and out of consciousness. Once she regained her faculties, she told me that you might be coming to see her. Mr. Shore, this is highly unusual. She's in a lot of pain and may not be in the right frame of mind to make these kinds of decisions about who to see, but she was fairly adamant that she wanted to see you if you showed up. I thought you'd be here sooner."

I didn't know how to respond at first. Nothing in my dealings with Carla ever gave me the sense that she trusted me enough to do this, to depend on me to this extent.

"Please, call me Tommy. Actually, I just found out about what happened today, through chance. I was looking at the newspaper and saw her husband's arrest notice. I don't know what transpired but took a shot that she'd be here. All I know is that he was booked on a domestic violence charge. Are you at liberty to tell me any more about what happened?"

She was watching me, deciding how much she wanted to or could say.

"Mr. Shore, this is not the first time Carla's been here. We've treated her a number of times over the years for a variety of injuries. All were inflicted upon her by her husband, but she's never allowed us to call the authorities. This was by far the worst incident yet, and the only reason I'm speaking to you about it is because she told me about your attempt to get her help, to get her out of that house. Normally, I would leave this to the police, but I'm not sure they have her best interests at heart. The fact that her husband is already out on bail indicates that. It required me to place a security guard outside her room until she's discharged. Which is a whole other matter. Where is she going to go and what will happen when she gets there?"

I understood these questions were rhetorical, that she wasn't really asking me. But the questions were on the money, and I had no idea what the answers might be. The best bet would be taking it a day at a time, but first I had to speak with Carla.

"Can I see her?"

She smiled for the first time since I entered her office.

"Of course. You are, after all, her cousin."

She got up, came around the desk, and stopped in front of me.

"Be aware, Mr. Shore, I'm breaking some fairly major rules here, in the hopes that you can help her. As a medical professional and a woman, it's been difficult keeping my anger in check, but I feel confident that you might be able to help. I don't know why, I just met you and I really don't know anything about you...just going on gut instinct here. Am I wrong?"

I shook my head but didn't say anything. She left the room, and I followed her down the corridor.

TWENTY-FIVE

We took an elevator to the third floor, then walked down two corridors to room 307. The hospital smells were nauseatingly familiar to me, and I found myself trying to breathe through my mouth as quietly as possible.

As we came down the hallway, I could see a large man sitting on a chair outside one of the rooms and knew this was the security detail Angela spoke of.

He was huge, 6'5" or better, and clearly a body builder. His shoulders were enormous, tapering down to a small waist and then tapering out again as his pants stretched over highly developed thighs. His head was shaved, and he wore a shirt similar to the one Angela had on, light blue with the hospital's logo on it. It fit him very differently.

He stood as we got closer and practically blocked the entire doorway. I saw him look at Angela and then at me, narrowing his eyes as he determined if I was a threat. Angela put her hand on his arm and said, "It's okay, Randy, this is Mr. Shore. He's here to help."

Randy relaxed a little and moved out of the way so we could go into the room.

It was a completely private room. I wondered how they could afford to put her in one but found out later that all of the rooms at the hospital were private. There was very little in there besides the bed, a side table, and a cheap chair, the kind usually found in hospitals that are meant to discourage anyone from getting comfortable.

Carla was asleep. I moved close to the bed and looked at her.

She was mostly covered by a thin sheet but I could see from her face that Vitter had really done a number on her. There were bruises on her cheek that looked like they ran down to her neck and were already turning dark purple. Her lips were chapped, and there were cuts on the area below her nose and on the bridge of her nose itself. There was a nasty cut above her left eye, which had been swollen shut when she came in but was now starting to heal a bit. The stitches across her eyebrow were still visible, and the skin around it had started to turn yellow. I felt myself balling my fists up. Angela must have noticed.

"Easy, Mr. Shore. She actually looks much better than when she first came in. You can't see them, but there are softball-sized welts all over her body, like he beat her with something. I can't imagine what he used to inflict that kind of pain on her."

I turned to look at her. I was having a hard time keeping the anger off my face.

"You said you had reservations about the cops. Can you tell me about that?" I asked.

"What I said is that I don't think that the cops have

her best interests in mind. I have been informed that Paul Vitter has ties to the head detective in Wallingford, and the fact that he made bail so quickly makes me uneasy about contacting them. I'm using the doctor/patient privilege as a shield here, but I'm not sure it'll hold up if they want to push it. Why do you ask?"

"I'm trying to determine who might know where she is. I'd like to take her out of here as soon as possible, as soon as you say she can be moved. I have someone who will find her a place to stay where she'll be safe."

She studied my face. I needed to convince her that she couldn't keep Carla safe while she was in the hospital, no matter how big her guard was. I looked her straight in the eyes and said, "Angela, when they find out she's here, you won't be able to protect her. Mr. Universe out there will not be able to keep them away from her if they want to get her. And they will want to get her."

The discussion was interrupted by a groan from Carla. We both turned towards her and saw that she had opened her eyes and was coming awake. I watched as she tried to focus on who was in the room. When she realized it was me, she tried to smile, but the pain from the cuts around her mouth made her wince and groan again. I heard her breathe in until it subsided and then slowly exhale. She started to cough. Angela moved past me to grab a cup with a bendy straw from the bedside table and placed the straw in her mouth so she could drink. Her eyes were moist from a combination of tears and pain. She stopped drinking, and I heard her softly say to Angela, "Tommy, alone?"

Angela nodded and left the room, and I watched as

she whispered something to Randy. Probably telling him to keep an eye on me. I turned back to Carla.

"Hey there. Looks like those karate lessons were a bad idea."

She laughed a little, but her hand came out from under the blanket and she waved me off. It hurt her to laugh. I apologized.

"Sorry. I fall back on jokes when I'm angry."

She motioned for to me to come closer, then pantomimed writing something. When her arms came out, I could see there were welts and bruises all over them. I handed her my note pad and pen. She wrote something then showed me. It said, "Get me out. Please."

I nodded and told her I was trying. I didn't know where I would take her or how I would get her there, but we both knew she wasn't safe here.

"Carla, I'm going to leave now and make some calls, see if I can put a plan getting you out of here in motion. I'll be back in a few hours. Randy will watch the door, and you'll be safe until I get back. Okay?"

Her eyes had gotten wide and she wrote on the paper again. "Please hurry," then whispered it to me in a rasp. I took the pad and pen from her and held her hand for a few seconds, being careful not to press on any of her bruises. "I will."

I walked out of the room and looked at Randy. I didn't say anything, but he muttered, "On it," to me, and I nodded.

As I walked down the corridor toward the elevators, I passed a linen cart and grabbed a pillow case. For later.

Leaving the hospital, I paused in the outer vestibule

from the lobby and tried to take in as much as I could of the parking lot. I wasn't sure if someone was watching the place, either Decker's people or the Knights, but no one ever got killed from being paranoid and too careful as a result.

I got to my car and started it, letting the air cool it down while I dialed Moreland. He picked up on the first ring.

"Shore. What's up? Where are you?"

I kept my voice steady and tried to remove the tone from my voice, but it was impossible.

"I'm at the hospital in Meriden, where Carla Vitter is lying in a bed, beaten to a pulp by her scumbag husband who almost killed her. But you already knew this, right, so my question to you is this: Why did I have to find out about it on my own? What happened to us working together as a team? Or is that a one-way street?"

There was a long pause, so I jumped in.

"Yeah, I thought so. Well, I'm gonna find Vitter and speak to him, in no uncertain terms."

"Shore, you do remember that I'm a cop, right? You can't threaten to hurt someone and expect me to just stand by."

"Didn't threaten anyone. Just want to talk to him. With extreme prejudice."

He didn't say anything. I took the opportunity to ask for his help.

"Listen, I need to get Carla out of here. She's not safe. I'm worried that Decker or Vitter or one of their guys is going to try to find her and hurt her even more. Can you help, can you find her a place to go?"

There was another pause until he said, "Give me an

hour. I'll make some calls and call you back, but Shore, you gotta stay away from Vitter. Just let me handle it. I can't have you trying to reenact some 'Death Wish' vigilante shit. There are bigger issues at play here for the greater good. We're trying to save multiple lives by stopping these guys. Understand?"

I told him I understood, hung up, and drove out of the parking lot.

TWENTY-SIX

It took everything I had not to head to Vitter's house to find Paul, but I knew that Moreland was right, that the timing was bad. It would have to wait.

Instead, I decided to go back to the *Record-Journal* offices and talk to Glenn Burnett.. I'd never heard back from him with any information that he might have uncovered, as he had promised he would do. There might not have been anything, but I wanted to make sure he hadn't forgotten about me.

My mind raced on the drive there. I was having trouble getting Carla out of my head and kept coming back to the welts and bruises on her body. I had seen that kind of pain before but pushed it far down into my psyche. Seeing her in the hospital opened the gates and brought all of those memories flooding back from my youth.

The household I finally landed in after having been tossed around the foster system until I was 12 was a place of anger and abuse. Until I ran away at 16, every day had been thick with tension, based upon the whims and drinking habits of the father of the house-hold. He was a mean, nasty son of a bitch and an alco-holic to boot. He took out his anger over an unrealized life on his wife and kids. I was protected because the state was paying him for me but had to stand by and watch him mistreat the other kids. I got big enough by 13 to warn him off the kids through the violence I pointed back to him. It worked toward saving the other kids for a while, but he ended up using my foster mother as his personal punching bag. It never happened when the kids were around, but I could always tell when he had taken out his frustration on her, usually spurred on by the bottle. The tension I felt coming home when that happened was what I was feeling now. It was difficult for me to control and had turned into violence a number of times before. By going to see the reporter, I was hoping to shift my focus.

The old guard from my last visit was still there, sitting in the same position at the table just inside the entrance. To my surprise, he remembered me.

"Looking for Burnett again?"

I nodded, and he reminded me that his office was on the second floor.

When I got off the elevator, there were a lot more people working there than the last time, including a woman who was sitting at a desk upfront. She smiled and asked me who I was there to see.

"Glenn Burnett. I don't have an appointment, but he'll see me. Tommy Shore."

She walked back to his office, and I could see them having a conversation. When she came back, she said he asked if I would wait. I looked back at Burnett and saw he was now on the phone. There was nowhere to sit, so I stood and waited.

He talked for a good 10 minutes, then stood up and motioned for me to join him. I got to his office just as his phone rang again. He put up a finger for me to hold off and started talking to the caller, motioning for me to sit in the chair in front of his desk. I watched as he furiously jotted down notes on a pad. From the answers he gave, I thought at first it was a robbery or a fire, someplace in Wallingford. Until I heard him ask "How many got hurt?," followed by an incredulous "16?"

He thanked whoever was on the other line and hung up. I started to ask, but he put his finger up again and punched in three numbers on his phone. I could hear it ring across the office space and then heard someone answer "Yeah?" Burnett told the person to come to his office immediately, and I could see out of the corner of my eye a guy rise from his desk with a pad and pen in hand and walk toward the office we were in, then stick in his head.

"What's up?"

Burnett tore the piece of paper he had been talking notes on from the pad and handed it to him.

"A bomb exploded in the automotive department of the Super Walmart on Route 5. There's at least 16 people hurt, and I'm not sure if there are fatalities. No one's taken any credit for the bomb yet. Go to the scene and see what you can find out. Pronto."

"Roger that." The guy went back to his cube, grabbed something, and then bolted out an emergency exit rather than wait for the elevator. It set off an alarm that made everyone jump, and someone rushed over to turn it off.

My mouth and throat had gone dry, and I could feel my face getting hot. Burnett noticed it and asked if I was all right. "You need water, somethin' to drink?"

I nodded and he got up and went to a nearby kitchen, coming back to his office with a plastic bottle of water. I took it and drank half of it before I felt I could talk. Burnett was still standing next to me, watching.

"What's going on? You know something about the bombing?"

I looked at him, trying to decide how much I could trust him. The fact that he didn't call me back the first time still irked me, but I thought what the hell, might as well hedge all my bets.

"I'm pretty sure the Knights of the Message will be taking the credit for it. They targeted the store previously when management began hiring people back from furloughs and felt that management shouldn't have been giving jobs to minorities, even based on longevity. Evidently, they felt the jobs should go to white people, regardless."

Burnett squinted at me.

"You're not telling me anything I don't already know. We covered that story. Ran in almost every Connecticut paper. But it's a leap from that to them doing a bombing. What makes you think it was them?"

"Off the record?"

He nodded.

I sat back and laid it out for him. How I'd stumbled onto the group when I was hired to find Earl Scosa. How Chris Lynde had followed me and braced me about what I knew. About finding Scosa's car and calling it in to the paper, knowing that Burnett would alert the cops while hoping that he'd investigate it further. About discovering that Paul Vitter, Scosa's brother-in-law, was not only an active member but high up in their organization, if they could be called that. About discovering Chris making pipe bombs at his place of business and calling the state cops about it, then watching Vitter and his cronies wait outside the Walmart for a guy that was inside. I left out Moreland's name as well as all of the Carla stuff.

Burnett was staring at me with his mouth open.

It was my turn to squint. "What?"

"Are you telling me that the state cops knew that Walmart was a target and didn't do anything about it, didn't warn people?"

I stared at him.

"Really? That's your question. No. Of course not. Nobody knew anything about what they were planning. The guy I saw them pick up at Walmart could have just been working there, getting off shift, and they were picking him up to go to one of their meetings. If there was any indication that they were gonna plant a bomb, the state cops would have acted on it. It's a stupid question."

That rankled Burnett.

"Stupid? Shore, you come in here and tell me all this shit about the Knights, and now a bomb has been exploded in the place that the state cops knew had something to do with their suspects, and you think it's a stupid question? What else do you know about these assholes?"

"I think Ron Decker is the head guy, in charge of the Wallingford chapter."

Burnett looked stunned. He was shaking his head, but I could see he was thinking it through. He didn't say anything for a minute, just stared at me, until finally, "Where do you get that from?"

I told him about watching the scene when I had found the car and how Decker had shown up so quickly, much faster than one would think it would have taken for the news to reach him. My theory was that he put the department on alert, that if anyone heard or saw anything having to do with Scosa, they were to contact him immediately. He needed to be at the scene in order to control it.

Burnett was still skeptical.

"I agree, that's unusual but it could also be totally coincidental. Doesn't prove that he had anything to do with the Knights."

I shrugged. "I've seen pictures of him leading a group of men in what clearly looks like a meeting of like-minded racists. There was also a guy there who was up from the North Carolina chapter of the Klan, to help organize it."

The look on his face was such that I almost took out my phone to get a picture of it. I stood up to leave. He shook off his surprise and used his hands to indicate he wanted me to sit back down.

"How do you know all this? What are your sources?"

I laughed at that. "Wow, talk about role reversal. Is this where I say those are confidential and protected?"

Burnett grimaced again. "Ya know, Shore, you're a schmuck. Why did you come in here again if all you wanted to do is crack wise?"

I felt my face flush again with anger.

"I came in here because I thought you might have some information that you'd be willing to share with me, after not getting back to me the last time I was here. I'd read that you used to be a good reporter who went deep on the subjects he investigated, but I can clearly see you're just going through the motions these days, so I'm out of here."

I turned and walked toward the elevators, then veered off and used the emergency exit. I could hear the alarm going off as I went down the stairs and out to the parking lot.

TWENTY-SEVEN

I decided to try to take a look at the Walmart scene. I couldn't come up with a solid reason for what I thought I might see, but I needed to do something, and it was all I had. I drove out of the newspaper's lot and headed down Route 5 until I got close to the scene, pulling into a nearby grocery store parking lot. From there, it would be possible to park and walk over to the Walmart, if I could do it without being stopped by one of the dozens of cops who would be there.

The area was well covered. I saw one guard near the cut-through driveway and decided I'd try him, walking over to attempt a conversation. There was yellow barricade tape everywhere, but I did what I could to maneuver around it and got as close as possible.

"Hey there, officer, how's it going?

He glanced at me quickly then looked away, assuming I was just a rubbernecker, then muttered, "Same shit, different shovel, bigger tide."

I laughed appreciatively. "What happened at the Walmart?"

When he looked back, he was smiling contemptuously.

"You writing a book?"

I found myself wondering if every cop on this police department was a first-class prick.

"No, just curious. I shop here all the time. Wanted to walk over and get some stuff."

"Store's closed. Accident. Probably be a few days."

I could see a lot more of the lot had been roped off by crime scene tape, and there were a number of people that were not cops who were walking around. I didn't see any ambulances.

"Anybody get hurt?"

He turned to face me now and started moving closer.

"You ask a lot of questions. Move along, or do I need to take you in for questioning?"

I put my hands palms out and shrugged, saying okay a few times, then moved backward towards my car. When I was fifteen feet away from it, I turned and sped up a little until I got inside. I glanced over and could see that another cop had joined the one I had been trying to talk to, and both were looking my way. As the second cop walked toward me, I started the car up and took off, keeping to the speed limit. I saw him in the rearview mirror, trying to take down my license, so once I got back to the main drag, I headed down some side streets until I got to the Merritt and started back toward New Haven.

Once on the parkway, I called Moreland but got his voicemail and left an urgent message that I needed to talk to him ASAP. I was just through the tunnel when he called me back. Before I could say anything, he said, "I heard about the Walmart. We're on it. Those photos you took of them picking up the guy from the store have been a huge help in identifying who might have done this. He must have been casing the place for the best locations to hide the bombs. We're looking at security tape now to try and figure out when they sent someone back there to place them."

I interrupted. "Bombs, plural?"

Moreland hesitated, then said, "They used three. One went off fully, one partially, and one didn't detonate at all. We're trying to figure out if these were ones made by Lynde. If so, it makes sense that something went wrong. If not, then there's somebody else out there working with these guys who know how to make this shit, even badly. We've doubled up our efforts to find out who that could be. I still need you to hang tight for a while."

I shook my head. I had pulled off the road after getting off the exit, into a Mobil station lot. I was having a hard time deciding how much more of this I could be involved in.

"Listen…I'm not sure what I can do for you. I can't get inside to any of the meetings, they know who I am. Paul Vitter probably wants to kill me, and the feeling is mutual. You're telling me the locations I know are involved are off limits. I gotta tell ya, my frustration levels are high."

I could hear him clearing his throat.

"Understood, Shore. But you gotta trust me."

I laughed and changed the subject.

"So, what have you been able to do about getting Carla someplace to go?"

"Well, it was tougher than I thought it was going to be, but we found a place for her in Stratford, a place called Emerge. It's highly rated and very private. Nonprofit. We've placed some witness protection people there in the past."

It sounded good, but I needed to make sure he knew about the past attempt.

"John, I need to be clear. She had a really hard time at the one I got her into here in New Haven. On top of that, the person in charge at the hospital says this kind of stuff has happened to her before and she keeps going back to him. I'm thinking she's a little more willing now to see him for what he is, but the place needs to be special. The people there need to treat her with kid gloves. I don't know a lot about this stuff but I know that the tough love bullshit she got at the last place was definitely the wrong way to go."

"Understood. My people say the place is great and should be perfect for her. Also, it's not that far away, just over the Sikorsky Bridge, maybe 10 miles from New Haven. You can easily go see her there, if and when they allow visitors."

I changed the subject back again.

"Okay, so what do I do now? The Walmart store was definitely the Knights. Once they come forward and claim responsibility, all bets are off. If they have something more powerful, they're gonna use it, maybe on one of those targets that was on the board in the picture."

I could hear him sigh.

"Shore, please leave the detective work to us. You're

done for now. If I need you, I'll call you. But stay away from Vitter and stay out of Wallingford, too. Hard to know which cops are on which team and what they'll do if they catch you driving around there. Look, I gotta go now, but I promise to touch base soon."

He hung up. I stared at the phone for a good 30 seconds. Touch base. Jesus. Now I was on call.

I needed a friendly voice, a voice of reason. I called Rosalind and was surprised when she answered immediately.

"Thomas!"

My stepmother and my ex-wife were the only ones whoever used my full name and usually when I was in trouble. When Rosalind used it, it made me feel like anything is possible.

"The one and only. Man, I miss you. When are you coming back to Connecticut?"

"I'm back. Took a red-eye out from L.A. and got in around six a.m.. Was going to call you as soon as I got home. I'm beat but I'd love to see you, catch up. How's this evening look? I can get some sleep this afternoon and be ready to go out by seven. Might be some jetlag but you're worth it. Doable?"

I laughed. "Very doable, if you think the jetlag won't knock you for a loop. It'll be tough to wait until then, but I'll find a way. I can make a reservation at Kala, that Spanish place we went to that you liked or maybe Italian. Pick you up at the house?"

She agreed, said she really missed me, too, and hung up. Just like that, things were okay again. For now.

TWENTY-EIGHT

It was already fairly late in the afternoon by the time I got back to the apartment. I was excited to see Rosalind. Like everyone else, there hadn't been much good in my life in the last months, and this felt like it could be the start of a turnaround. I also felt good that I had found some direction for Carla and hoped it was enough to satisfy the "white knight syndrome" that haunted me.

I decided on the ride back into town to take Moreland's advice and "hang tight" for a while. The whole Knights of the Message thing felt way above my pay grade and left a bad taste in my mouth. Like he said, better to leave it to the state cops to handle. These morons were crazy idealists with guns and badges, and there was no reason I needed to go back there. The time I'd spent in Wallingford wasn't enjoyable to me, save for some great barbecue, which I could easily get in New Haven. I didn't feel the need to go back there anytime soon.

Once home, I reheated a cup of coffee from the morning and stood at the stove drinking it. When I finished, I went into the bedroom and picked out what I was going to wear tonight. I was having second thoughts about the Spanish restaurant. She had been in California for a while, where Italian restaurants typically meant The Olive Garden. I decided on an old-school red sauce restaurant downtown, a place called Consiglio's. Checkered tablecloths, Chianti bottles that doubled as candles, and piped-in operatic music. Some found it corny, but they made it work and the food was great. I called and made a reservation. They had taken out some of the tables to enable distancing, and it was sometimes difficult to get in there, but they said they had a two-top available. I texted the change in plans to Roz and got back, "Perfect! I'll Uber there so you don't have to come all the way out here and back. See you in a bit. XXOO."

After a long shower, I got dressed and poured myself a double shot of the Irish. It went a long way toward relaxing me and kept the thoughts of the last few days at bay. I did some last-minute straightening up in case we came back here for a nightcap, then sat and read some of the news headlines on my phone. There was a story about the explosion but no details. Tomorrow's paper would have the complete story, and I was happy to wait until then.

At 6:40, I left the apartment to walk down to Wooster Street where the restaurant was. I hadn't been back on that street for a while, ever since a rough case that had ended in bloodshed just up the street from the eatery we would be at. I was thinking enough time had passed but that it might feel a little weird being there.

The heat had broken a bit, and the walk downtown was pleasant. There still wasn't the kind of busy traffic the city was used to, walking or driving. I went by a few places that were shuttered completely, having gone out of business during the pandemic. I was afraid there'd be a lot more coming down the pike.

Even though I was early by the time I got to the restaurant, Rosalind was already there, looking at the menu in the window. I got a huge smile when she saw me, and I was aware that I was doing the same. We hugged, gingerly at first. Both of us had grown used to not being able to touch other humans, and it was strange at first, but then we laughed and hugged for real.

Once inside, we were seated immediately at a small table on the side of the restaurant, away from the door but closer to the bathrooms than I would normally have liked. I started to say something, but she stopped me, saying it wasn't a big deal.

"Besides, it looks like the kind of place Michael would come out of the john with a gun in his hand, so we wouldn't want to miss that!"

I laughed at the "Godfather" reference and realized it was the first time I'd felt relaxed in weeks. When the waiter came over, he brought us a basket of bread that was still steaming from the oven and complimentary glasses of Prosecco. After hearing the specials, we ordered. Linguine with clams with a glass of sauvignon blanc for her, eggplant parmesan with a bottle of farm-house ale for me. I added some fried calamari as a starter, with red sauce on the side. The waiter nodded and left, and our date began.

Rosalind started telling me about being with her daughter in Los Angeles and about how strange it was out there during the lockdown. About the only time they went out, other than to grocery shop, was to walk on the beach or to the Santa Monica pier from her daughter's apartment in Marina Del Rey. How she got tired of thinking up new things to cook every day and how bad and expensive the takeout food was.

"Especially the pizza! A small pie with mozzarella could run over 20 dollars, and it tasted like something you'd get frozen in the supermarket. I really missed New Haven pizza...a lot! And I'm not even that much of a pizza lover!"

The conversation continued about their taking rides up the Pacific Coast Highway to Malibu, if only to look at the water or walk in the park near Pepperdine. I told her about my morning walks around New Haven, often in search of breakfast. My story paled in comparison.

Our order came, and it was a huge amount of food, as if someone had built a menu around the word "abundance." There would be enough for three days of leftovers. We dug in.

After a few minutes, she put her fork down, took a sip of wine, and asked me if I had a new case and, if so, what was I working on. I thought for a minute then decided to throw caution to the wind. I told her everything, starting with the phone call from Carla and ending with Moreland telling me to "hang tight." She listened without interruption, letting me rid myself of my ghosts. When I was done, she focused on Carla.

"Do you know what she's planning to do next? After the shelter?"

I frowned at the question.

"I'm not sure she's thought that through. I would imagine she might be able to go live with her sister up north, somewhere above Hartford."

Now it was her turn to frown.

"Tommy, you know I've been an ER nurse for a lot of years, and I've seen more than my share of horrible things. Things that would give most people pause at best or make them sick to their stomachs at worst. I will tell you that, after multiple gunshot wounds, when a woman comes in who's been battered, it's often so bad that it upsets every nurse working there for days. Some of it can be chalked up to 'There but for the grace of God'...but more often it's because you see the kind of pain that's been inflicted on one human being by another...and it completely breaks your heart."

I looked at her and could see this was difficult, as if she was remembering things that happened in her own past. I chose my words carefully.

"Anything you can tell me will be helpful."

She sat back and studied my face, then took a big sip of her wine.

"Okay, here goes. Domestic violence is often physical, but it can also be sexual and psychological. Mostly, it's about control, an abuser getting a woman to do what he wants. I say woman because it is mostly men abusing women. It certainly can go the other way, as well as with the elderly, but 99% of the time it's men abusing women."

She stopped and took another sip. I kept quiet.

"The changes in the laws are only recent, probably only going back to the early 70s. The cops still don't know how to handle it and often treat it badly. They're hesitant to get involved because too often the victims won't go through with the complaints. Lawyers also hate these cases, as do the judges. Most times it gets chalked up as a 'family matter' and isn't taken seriously.

When they do take it seriously, an abuser might only spend a day or two behind bars. And when they return home, there's the tears and the promises until the next time, which is often worse than the last time."

The pitch of her voice had risen noticeably, and I could sense she was getting emotional. I reached over and put my hand on top of hers. It elicited a tight smile and she said, "That's a story for another time." I nodded that I understood.

She frowned again and asked, "Does this Vitter asshole drink, is he an alcoholic? Most times there's some kind of substance abuse involved, and typically it's booze. You said there's a little girl in the picture? Child abuse can go hand in hand in these situations, and the kids always get the short end of the deal."

I nodded again.

"There's a little girl, Shana. She's six. Carla's sister was married to the guy she asked me to locate. That sister was killed in a car accident a few years back, and the brother-in-law was raising her as a single parent. He was supposedly a decent dad but had trouble finding work lately, so Carla was watching the little girl a lot of the time. I'm not sure where she's gonna end up...hopefully with the other sister."

Rosalind was looking down at her plate and shaking her head.

"It sounds ugly all around. I feel for her. It sounds like it's been a tough life."

She looked up and smiled.

"Hey, let's talk about nicer things. Or better yet, let's get these leftovers wrapped up and pay the check? It's a beautiful summer night out there. I'd love to walk a bit, then go back to your place?"

I smiled at her. "Without a doubt."

I signaled the waiter for the check. He brought it over and took away our half-eaten dinners to be wrapped up to go. When he returned, I paid, left a solid tip, and we left.

It was a beautiful night and we took our time on the walk back to my apartment. Neither of us said much. I imagined we were contemplating the night ahead but knew that we were both thinking about the conversation we'd just had about Carla in the restaurant.

I decided that I needed to ratchet up the timeline and would go see Carla at MidState tomorrow.

Until then, I would give myself over to being in the moment.

TWENTY-NINE

I took Rosalind out to The Study for breakfast the next morning. It was a trendy new hotel with a very good restaurant called Heirloom. Their late-night food menu tended to be a little too expensive and high-brow, but they had a reasonable breakfast. We split a stack of buttermilk pancakes, a side of delicious double-smoked bacon, and drank limitless cups of strong coffee.

After getting the rental out of the garage, I drove her back home to Hamden, and we made plans to see each other again in a few days. I kissed her goodbye, watched her go into her house, and then took the back roads until I got on I-91 toward Meriden.

I ran through my mind what Roz and I had discussed over dinner. I knew I needed to get Carla out of the hospital as soon as possible and into the shelter that Moreland found in Stratford. And while she was no longer my client, I was using the money that the state had given me as payment on her account.

When I pulled into the lot at the hospital, I noticed an unmarked police car sitting near the entrance.

Remembering what Moreland told me about the local cops gunning for me, I backed into a spot far enough away where it would be difficult to tell who I was. By the same token, I couldn't really tell if there was someone in the cop car or, for that matter, if it was from Wallingford or local. I waited and watched to see what it was about.

Ten minutes had gone by when the entrance doors slid open and Decker came out, accompanied by a uniformed cop. I couldn't tell if it was the same lackey who pulled me over, but he had that cock-of-the-walk gait that those guys affected. They both got into the unmarked with the uniform driving and took off out of the parking lot.

Looking at my phone, I noticed that I had missed a couple of messages, and when I opened them up, I saw Moreland had been trying to reach me. I called him immediately, and he answered his phone yelling.

"Shore, where the hell you been? I've tried you a dozen times. Your girl's gone. She got dressed and walked out of the hospital. Pretended she was asleep and waited for the guard to take a leak, then bolted. Did you know she was going to do that?"

I tried to gather my thoughts. My temples started pounding almost immediately. I had the fleeting thought that maybe I'm not cut out for this kind of work.

"How could I know? I'm at the hospital now. I was going to try and persuade her to move up the timeline and get her out of here and into the shelter. But Decker was here with one of his goons, so I waited to see what it was about. He and a uniform just left in an unmarked. No idea why they were here, unless someone let them know she was gone. I've got no idea where she might go."

"Well, security cameras say she went out the back and got into a car that was waiting for her. Couldn't see the driver's face, but you could tell it was a guy. Maybe some friend of hers. Look, I'm gonna get someone out to watch the house, but if she's smart, she'll stay away from there."

The fact that Decker was still out there was unsettling. I said as much. It was my turn for yelling.

"When are you guys gonna crack down on this thing? I thought you were making moves before they took the bombing to a new level. Decker's walking around like nothing's different. And what happened with the Walmart? Was that a Lynde special, or was it somebody new? Are you doing anything or just waiting until more people get killed?"

I wanted to convey my anger but could hear that it just sounded like I was scared shitless. Which was not that far from the truth.

"Shore, calm the fuck down. I can't talk about the Walmart situation or the Knights, but we're almost there. You know how it is with bureaucracy and red tape, it takes time. I can tell you that this will be resolved in the next day or so. So, at the risk of sounding like a broken record, hang in and stay out of sight. I've got people looking for Carla, and when we find her, I will call you and we can both take her to Stratford together. Okay?"

I rubbed my temples some more.

"John, you realize this feels wrong on about a hundred different levels. What, I'm supposed to just let this alone and not try and find Carla myself? What if

Vitter finds her first? He could kill her. These guys don't change. He will hurt her again. You might be willing to have that on your head, but I'm not."

Morehead spoke softer now, trying to pacify me. It was the right tactic to take.

"Tom, I promise you, this will have a happy ending. We'll find her and get her help. You just need to trust me."

Against my better judgement, I agreed. We left it that he would call me with any information he had and hung up. I sat there for a few minutes and was about to leave when I saw Dr. Bodine come out of the front entrance and start walking to her car. I left the space I was in and slowly rolled the car towards where she was headed. I didn't want to scare her and hoped she would recognize me. I rolled the window down.

"Dr. Bodine? Angela?"

She looked over and I could see her take a minute to figure out who I was. After twenty seconds, I saw her relax and she walked over.

"Mr. Shore. I assumed it was only a matter of time before you got word that she left and came to see me. I really don't have anything to tell you, other than she left here early this morning of her own accord, out an emergency exit where her husband was waiting, maybe 9:00."

My heart sank when I heard her say "husband." Moreland said they couldn't tell who it was, but that it was Vitter made my blood run cold.

"Is that what Decker wanted to know?"

She looked confused at the question, and I could see her wondering how I knew Decker had been here.

"He was just here, asking the same questions.

Evidently, Carla's husband is an old friend of his, and he's been trying to locate him as well. I told him just what I told you."

I thanked her and sped off, heading to their house in Wallingford.

I called Moreland back and relayed what I'd just found out.

"Are you kidding me? I haven't sent anyone to the house yet. I'll call you back."

He hung up as I drove down the Merritt. I could only imagine the kind of damage Vitter was going to do this time.

THIRTY

There was a fender bender right before the Wallingford exit on the Merritt so that by the time I got off it, much more time than I wanted had passed. I was hoping that they wouldn't be foolish enough to head back to their own house but knew that if they wanted to get some things before going on the run, they might chance it. I headed down Main Street toward the house.

As I got close, I could already hear sirens, and as I came around the corner from Carla's house, I could see the flashing lights of police cruisers. There were three of them, and two cops were already hanging crime scene tape.

I pulled over down the block and parked, trying to figure out next steps. My heart was racing, and I imagined that this time Vitter had finally gone too far. I watched as the cops went in and out of the front door. They would never let me get close. I redialed Moreland. When he finally answered, I told him where I was right now and what I could see was going on. He told me to sit where I was and wait until he got back to me.

I sat a while and watched. Another unmarked pulled up, and two more guys got out, plainclothes detectives. They spoke to two of the uniforms and pointed at the growing crowd of onlookers. The two uniform cops started trying to disperse the crowd but most lived locally and it looked to be a difficult undertaking. The crowd had grown to at least 50 people.

Twenty more minutes passed since speaking to Moreland, and he still hadn't called me back. I was starting to get angry until I saw him pull up to the scene and park his car just outside of where the tape had been strung. He was with another agent, and the two of them got out of the car and started pointing at some of the cops who were standing around. I could hear him barking orders and saw two of the cops get into their cruiser and leave.

The other agent went into the house, but I could see Moreland looking down the street, trying to spot me. I got out of the car and stood by it, and he signaled me to come down. I ran the half block to where he was standing, but when I got close to him, he put his hand up to stop me.

"Shore, Carla's fine. Vitter's dead. It looks like she took one of his shotguns and killed him with it. I'm going to take you in there to see her, but you are not to touch a thing, not her, not anything. It's a crime scene, and you should not be here. But I want her to talk to us, and I think seeing you might keep her calm. Understood?"

I nodded. He led the way up the stairs, and I followed right behind him. I was thinking that it was not that long ago I was walking up those stairs to talk with Carla about finding Scosa. Things had definitely changed.

I could smell the blood and the gunpowder even before I got inside the door but wasn't prepared for the scene inside. It was a bloody mess.

On the couch, in almost the exact spot where I'd seen Shana doing her puzzle when I first visited, sat Paul Vitter. There was no question he was dead. His eyes and mouth were open, and there were two gaping holes in his chest with blood spreading all over his tank top in widening circles. A thought passed through my mind that the shirt was often called a "wife beater." Huh. Not anymore.

There was even more blood further down, pooling around Vitter's crotch. The two shots to the chest had stopped him cold. The second two barrels were clearly used for vengeance. Blood had spattered over much of the couch, on each side of the body. There was more on the wall above the couch, and it had sprayed to almost the length of it. The room would definitely need repainting.

The other detective who had driven up with Moreland was standing near the television, keeping guard over the shotgun that sat on the floor. I assumed it was the murder weapon and tried to get a better look. I could see it was a unique four-barrel deal, with ornately engraved metal work on both the sides and the stock. It was a beautiful gun that was most probably special-ordered by the victim.

Moreland introduced the other guy as Sergeant Mackey and asked him if any other weapons were found. Mackey shrugged, saying, "Not down here, but I don't know if they searched the rest of the house yet."

I saw Moreland nod and then point toward the kitchen. Mackey nodded back.

I followed him in there. Carla was seated in her usual spot, looking out the window. She turned toward us when we entered the room, and a tight smile came across her face when she saw me.

"It's over, Tommy. He can't hurt me anymore."

I nodded and put my index finger to my lips. "Please don't talk, Carla. They're going to arrest you. I'm going to find you a lawyer, but do not say anything at all until you speak to her. Not a word. Promise me?"

She nodded and turned back toward the window. Moreland glared at me, but he knew I was right. He asked Mackey to call in the officers who answered the original 911 call to come back inside. Moreland had them come into the kitchen, and one of them read Carla her rights. When he was done, he asked her to stand up and turn around, but Moreland intervened.

"No cuffs. We're going to take her from here. She's a state's witness now.'

The officer started to protest, but his partner took him by the arm, led him out of the room, and out of the house. I looked at Moreland to see what he wanted me to do, but he was already helping Carla stand up. His demeanor toward me up until now had belied his ability to be caring, and I was surprised he could be so gentle with her. He grabbed a large kitchen towel off the counter so she could use it to cover her head. It would serve to keep her from having to look at the carnage in the living room again and also shield her face from the onlookers outside. He guided her through the living room and out to the car, looking back at me and saying, "I'll call you shortly and let you know where we take her. Make the calls and get her a lawyer."

I nodded again. It seemed it was all I could do lately.

Once we were outside, I watched as the police photographer went into the house, followed by two forensic guys, to process the scene and collect evidence. I figured them for state rather than local. I watched Moreland ease Carla into the back seat of their car, while Mackey got into the driver's seat. They backed out quickly, probably headed to somewhere downtown in New Haven.

I started to walk back to my car but stopped short when I noticed a Wallingford cop car parked directly behind my car. Standing next to it, I recognized the same cop who harassed me early on, back when I first left Decker's office and who had been with Decker at the hospital. I didn't have time for the hassle right now and tried to think what I could do. I looked over to my right, where a youngish black couple was sitting on their porch, watching the goings on at Carla's house. I approached them slowly.

"Hi folks. I'm wondering if you could help me. I suffer from the occasional dizzy spell and I feel one coming on now. That's my car over there, the black VW. Could you help me make sure that I can get to my car and get the door unlocked? My hands shake so bad sometimes, it can be really hard to maneuver small objects." I held up the key fob.

They both looked at the car, and their glances lingered. I could tell they were eyeballing the cop. The man of the couple spoke up first.

"You okay to drive? That cop might not like it, you needing my help getting into your car."

"Oh, once I get seated behind the wheel, I'll be fine. It's just low blood sugar. I'll eat a candy bar, and it'll all be good. Got one in the car, although might be a little melted by now."

They both laughed. He stood up and came over, reaching out to take my elbow. I played along and let him help move me to my car. He told me his name was Gerald. I could see that he was dying to ask me what happened down the block but didn't say a word.

We got to the car, and I could see the cop's face. He had on the same clichéd mirrored shades as before, so I couldn't see his eyes, but I could tell he wasn't happy. He got into his car.

Gerald had taken the key fob and opened the door, guiding me in. I got settled behind the steering wheel and reached over to the glove box as if to get the candy bar, feigning surprise that it wasn't there.

"Ah, damn, must have eaten it already. Guess I'll have to stop on the way home and get another one. Thanks so much for the help. More than you can know."

He looked back at the cop car and then back to me.

"Uh-huh. Guess I don't wanna know. You drive safe."

He started walking away, then stopped and turned back to me.

"Hey, can I ask you something? Can you tell me what happened in that house down the block?"

I smiled at him.

"What happened, Gerald? Justice, that's what happened. Thanks again for the help."

He moved back to the sidewalk, and I pulled out of the space slowly, expecting the cop to follow me until he thought he could pull me over somewhere that was out of anyone's sight. But as I watched him in the rear-view mirror, he pulled a U-turn and sped off in the opposite direction.

I swallowed hard and could feel an intense relief wash over me.

THIRTY-ONE

I took the side streets back to the highway, then headed toward New Haven. I took a slight detour when I got into the city, getting off at Trumbull Street and jockeying around until I came to the bevy of shops at the beginning of Whitney Avenue. I wanted to try a new Nashville hot chicken place that just opened. It was the brainchild of some of the local restaurant entrepreneurs. I admired the sheer bravery of opening a new place now, after what everyone had gone through. I was quite hungry. Bloodshed tended to have that effect on me, and I told myself that I needed to be on top of my game if I was going to find the right lawyer for Carla. At least, that was the current rationalization. I parked, went in, bought a hot chicken sandwich and a drink to go, then went back to my apartment.

When I got back inside my place, I looked around until I found the notebook I had kept for years, full of business cards and contacts. I opened it to the back pocket where I kept the most important numbers and rifled through the papers there until I found the name I wanted.

I had been married for just under 10 years, from the late 80s to the late 90s. The first three or four years were fine. By year five, she was already bored, and it manifested itself in constant overspending. I traveled a lot throughout New England, away for days at a time. When I would return, there was the inevitable day or two in bed and then more shopping. I didn't mind it at first, but it was getting harder and harder to keep up with the minimum payments on the charge cards.

By year six, things had definitely changed. She refused to get any kind of job. She wasn't actually trained to do anything, and I couldn't even convince her to take a retail job, if only for the discount. More often than not, I would come home from the road and find groups of Russian ex-pats in the house, discussing politics and drinking my booze.

It took four more years of that before we decided to call it a day.

The divorce attorney we used had been great, once she realized that I wasn't going to fight her about anything. She was part of a small firm in New Haven, along with two other women. One did real estate law, and the other one was a defense attorney named Sue Gaston, specializing in representing battered women. I had seen her walking around the office the few times that Irina and I went there to sign paperwork. I had been impressed by her "Moving Forward" spirit, and we made some small talk while we waited. I considered asking her out but wasn't sure if it was appropriate just then. After the divorce was final and enough time had passed, we had a few dinner dates.

But we never really clicked, and nothing ever came of it.

I found her firm's card in the back of my book and called the number. I wasn't even sure they were still in business, but the receptionist answered quickly.

"Gaston, Miller and Jacobs. How can I help you?"

I asked to speak with Attorney Gaston and gave her my name. After a minute on hold, she came on the line.

"Tommy! Been a long time. How are you? Do you need a defense lawyer?"

Playful. Or angry. I couldn't tell which.

"Hello, Sue. Yes, a long time. Wasn't sure you'd remember me. I'm doing okay. How have you been?"

I could hear her chuckle softly.

"Of course, I remember. You're not someone to forget. I've been good, Tommy. Busy. Too busy. New Haven's turned into the wild, wild west."

I really didn't have the time for small talk, so I cut to the chase.

"Good, good. Listen, I won't keep you long, but I'm doing private detective work now and have a client who really needs a great lawyer. She was in a bad marriage, and there were years of abuse. She finally had enough and killed him. There's more to it than that, but I promised to get her someone who specializes in domestic abuse cases and thought of you. Would you be available to meet with her and hear her out?"

She didn't hesitate and said she would look into it, asking me for the particulars of the situation. I gave her Carla's name, told her a short version of the story, and said I would get back to her with where she was being held as soon as I heard back from the state cops. I heard her exhale deeply.

"Jesus, Tommy, is nothing ever simple with you?"

I laughed.

"It's a good question...and the answer seems to get more complicated every day."

She laughed, and I promised to call her later that day with more information.

I ate the sandwich I'd bought and drank the drink. It had all gone lukewarm but was still tasty. The heat of the sauce they used made me break out in a sweat, and I decided that a shower would be a good idea.

When I was finished, I came out into the living room and looked at my phone. Moreland had called twice while I was in the shower, each call within 10 minutes of the other. I called him back immediately. He jumped right in.

"Shore, where are you now?"

He seemed agitated.

"I'm home, in my apartment. Why?"

He took a long beat before he answered.

"Listen, we got word from our inside guy that the Knights are making moves. They're nervous that all the attention on Vitter's killing is gonna come back on them, so they're moving up their time schedule. There are two targets. One is the superior court building in New Haven."

He abruptly stopped talking. It confused me.

"And the other?"

I could hear him clear his throat.

"The other is you."

The chill that ran down my spine was pronounced, and I could feel my hands get cold. I tried to say something but couldn't get my throat to work to swallow. Moreland continued.

"Tommy, I have two guys sitting in a car outside your apartment. They have photos of all of the members, but they're watching for anything, anything suspicious. I've also got people inside, looking for anything out of the ordinary. We're making sure we're set up to clear the building and the street if needed. My guys are down in the basement, checking out those secret apartments down there. They'll move up the floors as soon as they feel it's all clear. Everything indicates that, so far, nothing's been put in place yet."

I swallowed hard.

"So far? That's what you want to tell me? So far? There's a thousand people in this building and it's old. If a bomb goes off here, it would devastate this place and much of the block! And why me, what do they want with me?"

Moreland interrupted me before I could build to a frenzy.

"Shore, you're not telling me anything we haven't thought about. We're doing what we can without panicking the city. You need to stay calm and stay aware. They're looking for a scapegoat and they evidently blame you for this. I'll be there in a few..."

It was his turn to be interrupted. The intercom to my apartment buzzed. I told him to hold on and answered. It was Sam, the old man who acted as the doorman.

"Tommy, it's Sam. Just got a package delivered for you. You want to come and get it, or should I drop it at your door later?"

So much for the two guys outside, watching. I tried to steady my voice before I responded.

"No, Sam, leave it there. Actually, don't move it at all. I'll be right out."

I disconnected and asked Moreland if he heard it all. He had and was ordering his guys to come into the building. I hung up and ran out to the lobby.

THIRTY-TWO

I got to the front lobby at the exact time the two agents who had been sitting in front of the building did. The box was sitting on a corner of the oversized antique desk that Sam usually sat behind. A couple from the apartment complex had come downstairs and was asking Sam a question, so he had left the box where the messenger placed it. When he saw me, he excused himself to the couple and started to reach for it. I raised my voice loud enough to get his attention.

"SAM! Leave it where it is, and move away from the desk. Take those folks with you out the front doors. NOW!"

It was unusual for me to speak to him in anything other than a friendly, soft tone, so this told him immediately I was serious. His eyes got wide, but he did as I asked. The two agents stopped short as soon as they passed the second set of doors, which were still being held open by a doorstop to let fresh air in. I didn't recognize either of them, but one barked for me to go outside as well. The other agent waited for me to pass him then walked out after me. He headed down the sidewalk, and I could see him taking out a walkie-talkie and calling someone. It occurred to me that he didn't want to chance using it inside, in case the detonating device was radio-controlled.

Within minutes I could hear sirens approaching. The cops who had been watching the entrance moved everybody across the street to the front of the bodega. I was thinking it wasn't far enough, but these guys seemed to know what they were doing.

The first truck pulled up hard, with lights flashing and NHPD Hazardous Devices printed on the sides. Guess that works better for keeping the crowds calm, much better than if it said "Bomb Squad." The two guys who got out of the truck scrambled out quickly and went to the back of the truck, pulling two sets of protective suits out and quickly slipping into them. They had clearly practiced for this and were getting a chance to put it into action.

A second truck pulled up just as the guys in the first truck finished suiting up. This one also had the writing on the sides, but the bed held a rounded, metallic cylinder attached to a base, like a high-tech cement mixer. The disposal unit.

Two squad cars pulled onto College Street and blocked passage from Chapel. College is a one-way street that was partially closed during Covid-19 to facilitate more outdoor space for dining, so the traffic wasn't bad just then. But the later it got, the worse it would get. Two sets of cops got out of the squad cars and tried to clear people from the street.

Moreland pulled up a minute later and jockeyed his car over the sidewalk to get through, pulling directly in front of my building. He got out and came over to where we were standing, talking loudly to one of his guys first.

"How'd the guy get by you?"

"We spoke to the doorman. The guy came in through a side door, a resident's access. You need a pass key for it but the delivery guy evidently waited for someone to leave from that way and then slipped in. He found his way to the lobby, left the package, then went out the same way. Haven't had a chance to check for any video out there, to see if he had a bike or a motorcycle."

Moreland was shaking his head. "And we didn't think to have anyone watching that entrance?"

The agent lowered his head but didn't say anything. I took the opportunity to get in Moreland's face.

"John, tell me what the hell's going on here. Why are they making me a target?"

He visibly sighed and grabbed my arm, pulling me down the street and away from his agent.

"You pissed them off. My inside guy says Decker blames you for Vitter's death, for poking your nose into things. Evidently, that reporter you talked to has also been digging into them, and they've moved up their timeline. I was in the process of putting together a task force to take them down when I got your call. We have warrants for the arrests of pretty much all of them. This will also..."

He stopped short to watch as the two experts came out of the building, the first guy leading the way and the second guy gingerly carrying the package. When the onlookers who had gathered realized what was going on, I could hear an audible collective gasp and watched as people started to back away.

The first guy opened the door on the cement mixer receptacle, and the guy with the package placed it inside. They both backed up about fifteen feet, and we all watched as Bomb Guy One took some kind of remote out of his pocket and pointed it at the truck. Nothing happened for a few seconds and then we all heard a dull pop inside the machine. Whoever built the bomb must not have used much explosive or had put it together badly. Either way, I wasn't disappointed.

Moreland went over to the two bomb disposal guys, who had opened the cylinder to look at the remains of the device. I watched as they had an animated conversation, eventually turning towards me. Moreland signaled me to come over.

When I got to them, the lead bomb guy who carried it out from the building spoke first.

"It was a pretty basic homemade device. If you had taken the package into the apartment, it could have done some surface damage, but I don't think it would have done any real structural harm...but you'd be dead now."

The matter-of-fact way he said it shook me a little, and I had nothing to say in response, choosing instead to walk away from them and over to Sam. He was visibly shaken and was sitting on a chair in front of the Owl. I could tell that he was having a hard time catching his breath and looked around for help. An EMT truck had pulled up after the bomb squad arrived, so I ran over and asked them to come take a look at him. They brought oxygen and started to help him instantly.

I walked back to Moreland, who was now directing the local cops in clearing the traffic. It took a minute to get his attention.

"What's going on with Carla?"

He looked at me and grimaced. "She listened to you and hasn't said a word. I was hoping she might be able to corroborate some of the information we had about Vitter's comings and goings, but she shut down. Do you have a lawyer for her?"

I looked over, and the EMTs seemed to have the Sam situation under control. He waved at me, and I could see he was breathing on his own again. I nodded and asked Moreland if it was okay to go back inside. He said yes and followed me in. Once in the apartment, I grabbed the card from the table, wrote the information on a scrap of paper, then handed it to him. He looked at it quickly, then tucked it inside his jacket pocket.

"We'll talk to her and get her in to see Carla. Hopefully, she'll advise her that she can do herself some good by helping us. Given the past history of abuse, and if she gets the right judge, she could come out of this without too much pain."

I looked at him. "She's lost her sister, her brother-in-law, the care of her only niece, and now her husband. I'm pretty sure her pain meter is full up."

Moreland looked like he was going to respond but just said okay, then headed out, tossing over his shoulder that he would call me later that night.

I locked the door behind him, went over, grabbed the bottle of Jameson and a glass, sat down on the couch, and poured myself a double, trying to slow my own breathing down.

THIRTY-THREE

The booze worked its magic, and I fell asleep for four hours. When I awoke, it took me a while to get my balance back and remember where I was. The events of earlier in the day still rocked me.

I staggered over to the kitchen island, found my cell phone and Sue's business card, and started to dial; but when I looked at the clock on the stove, I realized their office was probably closed by now.

I called Rosalind. I didn't tell her about the bomb or that the Knights had targeted me. I figured there would be enough time for that story eventually, in person and after enough time had passed. I knew she could tell the state I was in by the tone of my voice, but she didn't push it. Instead, she asked me about Carla.

"We're you able to convince her to go to the shelter?"

I took in a deep breath but must have hesitated a beat too long.

"What is it, Tommy? What's wrong?"

I let out my breath and told her what happened.

She listened without interruption. I thought I heard sounds like crying but must have imagined it, projecting my own angst onto her. When I was done, neither of us said anything for a while until she cleared her throat and started to speak.

"Tommy. You can't blame yourself for this. It had to end one way or the other. I'm not close to this other than from what you told me, but I'm very happy that it was him and not her. Everything you said made it clear that there was absolutely nothing redeeming about him. This would have gone on until it no longer did."

I knew she was right but couldn't shake what I was feeling. Some of it might have been the whiskey in my system, but I kept thinking that if I had been more forceful and insisted that she leave the hospital, if I'd made her come with me to the shelter, she wouldn't be looking at the possibility of life in prison. On the other hand, I also knew that the last thing she needed was another man trying to make her do what he wanted her to do. I tried to change the subject.

"Hey, when can I see you again?"

I heard her chuckle. "Ah yes, deflection and misdirection. We just saw each other. What, you can't get enough of me?"

It was a gentle tease but we both knew that it was getting close to the truth. It had been a long time since I'd felt this way about anyone.

"Nah, just like having someone else to eat with so I don't finish all the bread myself. It's purely for health reasons."

She laughed out loud this time, then lowered her voice, affecting a serious tone.

"Tommy, you need to be okay that you did what you

could for her. She made a choice, even if she was forced into it. From where I sit, you did more for her as a perfect stranger than most of the people in her life ever did."

My phone buzzed. I could see another call coming in, although I didn't recognize the number. I asked her if I could call her back, and she agreed. I hung up and switched over to the other call. It was Mackey, the state cop who had been at the scene with Moreland.

"Mr. Shore, this is Sergeant Tim Mackey with the state police. I was at the Carla Vitter crime scene a few days ago with John Moreland."

"I remember. Call me Tom or Tommy. How can I help you?"

"Tom, John asked that I call you and bring you up to speed on what's happened since you last saw him. My understanding is that there was an incident in New Haven at your apartment?'

An incident. I let out a small burst of breath before I could stop it.

"Sure, if you call an attempt on my life without regard for dozens of other lives an incident."

"No, of course. My apology, I didn't mean anything by it. Just wanted to let you know that I've been brought in on what happened. Anyway, John asked that I call and bring you up to speed. There was a raid at the location where the Knights of the Message typically meet. As expected, there was an exchange of gunfire and some casualties, including Ron Decker."

My heart sank with the possibility that Moreland was one of the casualties.

"And John?"

"Detective Moreland sustained injuries to his

shoulder and to his hand but is okay. He's at Yale-New Haven, recovering from surgery."

Getting information out of this guy was proving to be difficult. I hated his officious "just the facts" demeanor and struggled to keep my cool.

"You mean he got shot? You said casualties...did any of your other guys get killed?"

He hesitated, not sure what he could tell me. I could tell he was uncomfortable with this part of the job. "We had no casualties."

"Well, that's a relief. Will they let me see John in the hospital?"

"Immediate family and top brass, that's all I'm at liberty to discuss."

"Of course it is. And I'm betting you can't tell me anything about Carla, either? Like if John had the time to contact the lawyer I recommended?"

"We did contact Attorney Gaston. She's here now, meeting with her. Seems to be on the ball. Probably going to get bail posted shortly."

That stopped me. Having her out on the street opened up a new set of problems, like where she was going to stay. I needed to make other calls.

"Where's 'here'?"

I didn't expect anything and got what I expected.

"I'm not at liberty to divulge that information to you."

I sighed with frustration.

"Sergeant, I appreciate you calling me and everything that you were able to tell me. Please relay a message to John that I hope everything is okay. I'm sure he'll call me as soon as he can."

We hung up and I exhaled loudly. I hadn't been aware of just how tense I'd gotten.

I tried Sue Gaston's office again, with the thought that I would leave a message. She picked up on the second ring.

"Sue Gaston."

"Sue, it's Tommy. I figured you were out and just heard you were with Carla. Didn't expect you to answer."

"Hi, Tom. I always rout the office calls to my cell phone when I leave the office, in the event of just this kind of emergency. 24-7."

"So, how is she?"

"Under the circumstances, she's doing okay. I'm getting her out on bail. I know a sympathetic judge and the state police have let me know quietly that they won't fight me on it. She's not a flight risk, but I do worry about her mental state. I would like to find some place where she would feel safe and could be watched."

I told her about the shelter, and she said she would make inquiries. She knew about the melee with the Knights and what happened to Moreland.

"It's good for Carla," she said. "This kind of thing that her husband was involved in will help me make the case that she felt in constant danger both from Vitter and from outside sources because of his relationship to the Knights. I won't say that self-defense is a complete defense but it's the best one we have."

I thanked her for taking the case. I didn't ask how she expected to get paid, but it wasn't my business and just assumed she was doing it pro bono. She promised to call me later with any news.

I paced around the kitchen area a bit, looking into

the refrigerator a few times without deciding on anything. I was aware that I didn't handle helplessness very well, and when I felt that way, it often ended badly.

I decided to leave the apartment and sit outside at Trinity. I considered that a few drinks and the possibility of society might help, but I wasn't very confident.

THIRTY-FOUR

The patio at Trinity was surprisingly busy, but I was able to snag a table outside, close to the street. They were still trying to practice social distancing, and the closest table was a solid six feet away, but I didn't feel comfortable lighting up a cigar quite yet. I didn't want to deal with the sneers or the sidelong glances. It was bad enough with what you got when you didn't wear a mask, even outdoors.

Trinity had set up a system where you could hold your phone over a decal on the table, snap a picture, and their menu came up. You could order right from that site. I shook my head each time I used it, lamenting the death of the service culture. Still, I held my phone over it and did what I was told. I ordered a Guinness and two double shots of Jameson.

I looked around to see who was sitting outside with me. Most of the other tables were couples that seemed to be having a good time. There were one or two other singles, most likely students, with their faces buried deep inside laptops. I made a mental note to bring Rosalind here one of these days.

I was sipping on the second Jameson when my phone rang. I didn't recognize the number but decided to answer.

"This is Tommy."

I heard some throat clearing and shuffling. In the background were the sounds of other voices but no one spoke until I finally heard, "Shore. It's Moreland."

His voice was raspy, like he had just come out of a deep sleep with a dry throat.

"Detective. You sound awful. Mackey told me a little about what happened. You're doing okay?"

He laughed. "Yeah, okay. Took a bullet. Left you, went out to Wallingford to arrest the Knights. Got away from us. Turned into a firefight. An old-fashioned shoot-out. That place you saw them go to after the Walmart, when you followed them. There."

He was speaking in short sentences and slurring his words. He sounded like he might have still been high from whatever they gave him for the pain.

"Jesus. Near the barbecue joint. What happened?"

"It turned out to be a shit show. Our guy inside let us know that they were going to be there, meeting about targets. Decker assigning who would take what building, that kind of thing. Of course, he would never do the dirty work himself, would never sully his hands. Plausible deniability. We knew we had to take them down when we did. We had surprise on our side, but like I said, it turned into a firefight. I caught a bullet in my shoulder."

"Thought Mackey said you got hit in the hand, too?"

He laughed, then started coughing. I waited until he had it under control.

"Nah, when I got hit, I started to fall and put my hands out to catch myself...there was an empty beer bottle that I landed on and cut myself pretty good. But I'm going with the line-of-duty story."

It was my turn to laugh.

"Sounds about right. "The Gang Who Couldn't Shoot Straight" meets the "Keystone Kops." Maybe they'll give you a medal."

"Shit, I'd rather have a Starbucks gift card."

Lindsay came over with my second beer. I winked at her, and she laughed at me.

"So, what now?"

"I heal up and then a mountain of paperwork. There's a lot to this case, and it'll take some time to get all of the ducks in a row."

"I'll bet. And what about Carla?"

There was a pause.

"Listen, Shore. The lawyer you got her, my understanding is she's pretty good and that she already got her bail. Rest assured that I'll stay true to our deal and get her into the shelter if that's the way it turns out. But she killed her husband, and I can't say she won't have to do some time for that."

I looked off towards the sky that was peeking through the buildings.

"Understood. You've been more than fair with me, and I know you've helped her. I appreciate it."

I could tell he was getting tired and asked him to call me when he was out of the hospital, that I would buy him a beer. He laughed, said he would, and we hung up.

I watched the street for a while. There had been a few articles in the *Register* lately about the growing homeless problem in New Haven, but I hadn't really noticed a huge change from before. Now, I watched as five panhandlers worked both sides of the street, each with a different schtick. I waved off most of them until I saw Margaret walking down towards me.

Margaret was a fixture in New Haven. Dubbed "The Shakespeare Lady," she had been a presence on the streets of New Haven since the early 80s. Having earned degrees from some tony college in Vermont, she came to Yale with thoughts of becoming a theater director, but it never came to fruition. A series of breakdowns and subsequent mental issues put a stop to her dreams, and she took to the streets, giving impromptu street performances. Her first love had always been Shakespeare, and she seemed to have committed his entire canon to memory. But she could also recite Chaucer, Euripides, and scores of others, even acting out the parts as she recited them.

She gave me a big smile when she saw me. I doubted she knew my name, but I had given her money before and always listened to her while she recited something as part of the exchange.

She was wearing a makeshift mask that looked like it had once done duty as a Christmas stocking, green with little white snowmen and angels crocheted into it. She didn't pull it down right away, and I waited as she moved away from me, convulsed by a nasty cough. When it was over, she came close again and pulled the mask down.

"Hey there. It's you. Whattya wanna hear? Shakespeare, right? You're a Shakespeare guy."

I nodded and took out a five-dollar bill. "Your choice, Margaret. Whatever you want."

That got me a big smile, and she stepped back again, looked into my eyes, thought a minute, and belted out:

> "How oft when men are at the point of
>   death
> Have they been merry which their
>   keepers call
> A lightning before death: O, how may I
> Call this a lightning? O my love! my
>   wife!
> Death, that hath suck'd the honey of thy
>   breath,
> Hath had no power yet upon thy beauty:
> Thou art not conquer'd; beauty's
>   ensign yet
> Is crimson in thy lips and in thy cheeks,
> And death's pale flag is not advanced
>   there.
> Tybalt, lest thou there in thy bloody
>   sheet?
> O, what more favour can I do to thee,
> Than with that hand that cut thy youth
>   in twain
> To sunder his that was thine enemy? "

It floored me. I knew I was reading into it, but it felt like she had reached into my chest and touched a nerve nearest my heart. I finished my drinks, paid the check, and started for home.

EPILOGUE

It had been three months since the attempt on my life and the subsequent raid on the Knights of the Message headquarters.

I was once again sitting on the patio at Trinity, nursing a mug of hot coffee, tempered with a shot of Jameson in it. The weather had turned cold quickly, and it was now brisk enough outside in early November for me to need layers, a light sweater and a black corduroy coat I'd had for years. It felt like it would be a rough winter.

I hadn't done much in the time that had passed. There was a week's work taking pictures of a cheating husband and another week trying to locate the family of a guy who skipped his bail. The bondsman had been introduced to me by Sue Gaston, and we hit it off, recognizing shared vices like Irish whiskey and fine cigars. When it was over, he promised he'd throw more business my way, but I hadn't heard from him in a month.

It didn't matter. I was still processing all that had gone on.

There was a trial for the remaining Knights. I attended a few sessions, mainly to see how Moreland was doing. He was always pretty busy during the ordeal, and we never really got a chance to talk.

I saw him outside the courthouse once. We nodded to each other, but he had too many people around him and we couldn't speak. He held up his still bandaged hand and smiled broadly at me. I nodded and smiled back.

Carla's trial was another circus altogether. The DA wanted to make an example of her and tried to make the case that most women who kill their husbands claim abuse, but it was pretty clear from the start what kind of an evil thug Paul Vitter was. It ended with a hung jury mistrial.

I heard later from Sue that Carla never went to the shelter and ended up going to live with her sister in Windsor instead. The sister evidently had a big house there with lots of bedrooms and 10 acres of land. The sister had also petitioned for custody of Shana, and the courts had granted it. I was pleased when I heard that. It would be a good environment for both of them.

We only spoke once in the aftermath, when she called me to say thank you and to let me know she appreciated everything. I told her I would help her in any way I could if she ever needed to call me, but the words rang hollow, even I was saying them. She would spend the rest of her life trying to come to terms with what happened, and I knew I would never hear from her again.

I was seeing Rosalind pretty regularly, at least once

a week. Her shifting schedule at the hospital was difficult to keep up with, but we were both flexible. We
either went out for dinner or one of us would cook
something, then watch a movie or read. We had gotten
very comfortable with just being with each other, a new
experience for me.

New Haven was a completely different story.

As predicted, a number of businesses failed after
the pandemic. People were scared and slow to come
back to their old habits, and the bars and restaurants
struggled. Stores that had been open since the 1950s
shut down, and most of the people who lived just
outside the city stayed away.

Yale made accommodations for their students to
attend classes virtually when the new school year
started; but the college was a city unto itself, and
without the 20,000 folks that were involved with the
school in one way or another, the lack of people had a
far-reaching effect.

There were fewer street folks around now. Most
were trying to find a place to hunker down and stay
warm, but the regulars still roamed the streets.

Once again, I could see Margaret coming down
Orange Street from where I sat, pushing a small grocery
cart overflowing with clothing and open packages of
food and unidentifiable other stuff. She was bundled up
pretty good and wore an old leather hat with flaps. I
hadn't seen one like that since I was a kid. I waved at
her, and she came closer.

She seemed somewhat more confused than the last
time I saw her, and she kept looking over her shoulder
like she was watching for something. Her cough hadn't
improved much.

"What's the good word, Margaret?"

She narrowed her eyes at me and blew a raspberry.

"There are fewer good words than are known in your philosophy, Horatio."

I laughed at the reference, then took out the last four singles I had and handed them to her. She looked the money, pursed her lips, and said, "What'll it be?"

"As always, I'll leave it up to you, Margaret. Your choice."

It made her smile, but I could see she was having a hard time putting her heart in it. She stepped back, closed her eyes, and then recited:

"Our doubts are traitors and make us lose the good we oft might win by fearing to attempt."

I nodded. There were goosebumps running down my back, and I needed to sip my coffee to get my voice back. But when I turned back towards her, she was headed away from me, back into the city.

I tipped my head back and waited for a little sunshine, hoping it would come soon.

ABOUT THE AUTHOR

Lawrence Dorfman has more than thirty years of experience in the bookselling world, including stints at Simon and Schuster, Penguin, and Harry N. Abrams. He is the author of the bestselling Snark Handbook series including *The Snark Handbook: Politics and Government Edition*, *The Snark Handbook: Insult Edition*; *The Snark Handbook: Sex Edition*, *Snark! The Herald Angels Sing*, and *The Snark Handbook: Clichés Edition*. He lives in Hamden, CT with his wife.

Made in the USA
Middletown, DE
18 September 2022

10551527R00151